Needs Must

Fred Fox

FIRST EDITION

ISBNs:
Paperback: 978-1-80227-867-5
ebook: 978-1-80227-868-2

Dedication

I dedicate this book to my perfect grandparents, HARRY AND DOLLY HARROWING, and my loving parents, CYCIL WILLIAM and DAISY ISABEL FOX.

Contents

Introduction

This is the story of some of my family and probably most others, to a large degree. Circumstances differ, but we are all struggling for the same causes. Everyone's life and style mean everything to the individual, family, or nation and are adapted to suit the times in which they live. The level of religion or belief is ever-changing with each generation. From poor and humble to rich and extravagant, all equally important to the times they were living in. Family love and feelings are constant emotions. Brotherly love and protection are also of major importance right up to and even after death, generation after generation. The value of money or precious metals, possessions, experience and thrills is also ever-changing in importance and value. But the value of love remains constant throughout and is hopefully shown in this book from humble beginnings to adapting to modern and different forms of wealth and expectations.

My own family, parents and grandparents were all uppermost in my mind. I love and respect them all.

They lived, loved, fought and struggled till the end, everyone doing what they had to - no matter what or how - for the good of us all. "NEEDS MUST."

Readers may perhaps be shocked by some of this book; however, I wrote it as honestly as possible, pulling no punches about my own behaviour. I am obviously the black sheep of the family. A few names have been changed.

I had a great life and a wonderful childhood, always feeling loved.

These are my beloved grandparents' phrases that are located throughout the book.

Harry's rendition of Old Man River, he just keeps rolling along.
Old Sam's barrow had a pig.
How many beans make five?
Don't break what you can't mend.
Feed all the animals before you feed yourself.
Don't be mean to animals or land, or they will both be mean to you.
To plough with a horse 1 acre a day, walk 10 miles and 10 hours.
It's an ill wind that blows no one any good.
Dogs look up to you, cats look down on you, but pigs are equal.
A ewe's fart is worth two cow shits.
Sing us a song, Jack.
Don't tell your father.
Harry's pit stop pony.
Don't employ a pipe smoker.
Tea in a saucer with butter on.
Always look for the good side.
There's worse things at sea.

PART 1

Chapter 1

It was June 1880. The carts and wagons creaked along at their usual two or three miles an hour; at least the slowness of pace meant limited wear and tear on the wagons. They contained all the worldly goods of their occupants, and tethered to the near of each cart would be a few horses or ponies for trade.

At around ten miles and a half away, there was a day to go to reach the next town on their annual route from one horse fair to the next. At every turnpike or so, yet another family would join the procession that was becoming a moving village.

Little was said, even though most were known to one another. This was a low-expectancy life - an existence more than a social event. These people were among the most knowledgeable horsemen in the land. All needed to earn enough to live and improve their stock in the next three or four fairs.

They would finally arrive in London, where they expected or hoped to sell to the vast city market as demand for horses was at its greatest, horses being the only transport for all classes. Hay and mangles would also be gathered on the way to feed an ever-increasing need. One way or another, enough money was needed to be made at the final venue to enable the return to the four corners of southern England and start the whole process over again.

Although physical and character hardness were a necessity, all other expectancies were low. To exist was a success in itself. There were few luxuries available and certainly no labour-saving devices to cause discontent. It took little to keep these people happy. The instinctive need for the love of a wife or husband was the strongest emotional drive, coupled with the need for family. They longed for children to follow in their footsteps, therefore, extending their contact with this life beyond their own graves.

Two carts were near the front of this train, one with a tent on for living in, the other loaded with horse feed, being dutifully followed by half a dozen horses for trade. These were the total belongings of Henry and Sara and their five children. Henry was a typical small, hard Romany, as dark as an Indian. Sara was similarly weather-beaten, small and thin, but far from frail. She knew her place and loved Henry without question. He was right, well, someone has to be, and women at this time were seldom allowed a final say or the privilege of decision-making.

Life has become harder every year. Bargains in the way of cheap horses were scarce - even those in poor condition that needed to be built up to a good, sellable state. The number of dealers requiring them has increased, leading everyone to pay more for quality stuff, leaving little profit on resale.

With this, rivalry increased. Several times, Henry had sent his two older boys, Sid and Alf, scampering off sometimes a day or two in front to sort out possible buys and contacts before the main onslaught arrived. This action had its problems.

Only the year before, Henry's oldest son Sid had been caught on his own by a rival family. He was badly beaten in what could be termed as a latter-day turf war, left with a leg and ribs broken, as well as the usual cuts, bruises and tooth loss. Hospital and doctor treatments were not an option for most, so the leg got put into a crude splint. It would always be misshapen and fractionally shorter, meaning a lifetime limp. It happened two days before the family caught up and eventually found him. Other than the feeling of shame and not being able to contribute as much towards the family's needs, Sid soon recovered. Setbacks and problems had to be accepted; other things were far more important.

Sid was particularly tough. He knew no one would face him alone; he had nothing to prove and bore no malice - just a maturity beyond his years. Tom, the third son, was of a wilder nature and would wait like a coiled spring for any chance of revenge; he accepted nothing. Harry was the youngest boy. Since birth, he was always poorly; no one thought he would live more than a year or so, but he was now four and hanging on. Alf was the second boy, and he was different again. He was a thinker who didn't often share his thoughts, but he left no stone unturned and sought sensible solutions for every and anything. He was the ideal companion for his older brother on their business sorties; few mistakes would be made with Alf around. Ruth was the only girl at this time, although, when spending her time assisting her mother, she was treated like another boy.

Henry looked around his family and fixed his gaze finally on Sara, the wife he loved, without realising how much, who loved him despite his bullying ways that he was also not aware of. He was, after all, what his father had been and what was normal for the time.

Although nothing was said, even Henry realised Sara was newly pregnant again.

Since being a boy, Henry had created business contact with several farms and states, one of which was now about a day and a half away. Sid and Alf

were duly sent off ahead to make contact and prepare the groundwork ready for their father's arrival.

"Don't break what you can't mend."

The Aston estate was owned by retired Colonel
Mathews and managed by John Burrows. Both
held Henry and his family in high regard as
horsemen.

The boys arrived, found John Burrows and carefully described their stock and their father's needs.
With this done, they were put up above the stables
for the night.

They rose as usual at the crack of dawn to help
with general stable and yard duties. This was not so
much a goodwill gesture but more a sense of duty.
They had been brought up well, never expecting
anything for nothing, and this was to hold the family in good stead in the future. Colonel Mathews
had twice before tried to tempt Henry to stay and
work on the estate, seeing these boys as an excel-
lent labour force for years to come.

That morning Henry and the procession had
reached the bottom of Aston Hill. It was a two-and-
a-half-mile pull up into the Chiltern Hills, winding
through the vast beech woods. They would rest here
as they were only a couple of hours from the next

fair, so now was a good time to clean and prepare their stock for a good impression the next day.

While this was being done, Henry took off to meet John Burrows and the Colonel. The Colonel had several cards up his sleeve. On the one hand, he had some older horses to move on that would serve a better purpose, gently pulling a carriage around London, than struggling on with the non-stop heavy farm duties of ploughing. He also knew, as Sid and Alf had told him, that Henry had some ideal replacement on the face of it - an ideal trade. On the other hand, too many useful deals for Henry might mean the Colonel would not achieve his ultimate goal of enticing Henry into his employment. Too hard on Henry, and he might lose out with at least some of the boys being offered regular work elsewhere. The fairs were also a form of an employment market, and pressure was regularly put on the pick of the lads by the land owners all around.

Honesty is the best policy, and honesty had served both Henry and the Colonel well in the past. In all their dealings, the Colonel would come clean, explaining his position and exposing his desires. However, he also dwelled heavily on the fact that he would not always be in a position to deal with Henry as his need for horses or horse sales was like everyone else - very irregular. He was breeding more horses himself, so this could be the last time any deals of advantage for either of them might be possible.

Without Henry giving a reply either way, they conducted their deals and swaps. All the while, he was having the thoughts he had had two days ago when he had looked around his family. He recognised increasing hardship and insecurity in all their faces, and the duty of his family's well-being weighed heavily on Henry, especially with another baby on the way.

The relationship he had established with the Colonel and even John Burrows would alter should he become an employee. On the other hand, the thought of the cottage that came with the job, tucked under the hill with its welcoming roof to comfort all inside, was an instant answer to a lot of problems. It could prove a lifesaver for little Harry and the yet-to-come baby.

No word had been spoken or even expected between possible employer and employee for a couple of hours. When business and toing and froing of horses were complete, Henry turned to the Colonel and said he would talk to his family. After the final fair in London, he would call on his return journey with his decision.

The Colonel realised this was a ruse to gain time. He knew Henry was a very insular man, and as for talking to his family, well, let's just say that talking was not his strong point.

The Colonel watched him go, the boys leading the horses.

John Burrows turned to the Colonel and said, "He will be back."

The Colonel just nodded in hopeful agreement.

Chapter 2

At first light the following morning, all the wagons were on the move. By 6 am, they were all in the village of Chapelwood, coming from all directions in what would appear to an onlooker as a disorganised jumble. In fact, everyone knew their spot. Pecking orders and long-standing agreements had been established. No one wanted an unnecessary confrontation, as fights would be particularly vicious. Win or lose, the personal damage could be irreparable.

The village was small, with a large trading green in the middle. It gave the appearance of having as many ale houses as it did dwellings.

By 7:30, the children and younger men were parading their horses and ponies, showing off their paces to the already gathering groups of locals, farmers and onlookers. A lot of lifting hoofs, looking in mouths, feeling down legs and talking would go on for hours. However, as usual, no deals would be struck until after midday, when all angles and aspects of bartering had been explored.

There were many groups of men, all hopeful of gaining employment - some having walked up to fifty miles and some willing to accept anything rather than walk home to nothing but poverty. There were plenty of prospective employers, but they knew the score: they had all the advantages and would use them. Farmers with estates, carters, butchers, blacksmiths and storekeepers, in fact, everyone was more than happy to take advantage of the abundance of very cheap labour. As he watched, the knowledge of this played on Henry's mind, knowing that employers as good as the Colonel were very few and far between. What Henry did not know was that the Colonel knew exactly what he needed and the full worth and knowledge he would be gaining if he managed to employ the Hardy family.

By mid-afternoon, Henry and the boys had sold three of the smaller ponies - enough to keep the family for the last part of the journey.

Running through the day, starting mid-morning, there were the usual Romany games and wrestling. One of the most competitive events was the hop, step and jump, starting from a standstill straight into the hop, then step, finishing with a jump landing heavily. This needed some explosive leg work. In his day, Henry had been a champion at a number of fairs, but now too old, he had handed over to Sid, who was showing great promise until his damaged leg. Now it was up to Tom to take advantage of the small wagers the family were always willing to make. After all, in his younger days, Henry had often won more at fairs than he had made through his horse dealing. He hoped Tom would come good and aid the family finances. Still young, Tom would need all his natural aggression and wild, confident arrogance to pull it off. Then fate played its hand. The hunger to right a wrong and gain revenge was suddenly in his mind. He had justice on his side and the chance to restore the family's honour.

Fast emerging as his opponent in the final was none other than the main young man responsible for Sid's beating and damaged leg, the brother he so looked up to. That brotherly love suddenly came out in abundance. He was up for anything; he was now unbeatable. Tom flung himself down the avenue, bawling onlookers urging him on; even their voices seemed to lift him. As he landed, he knew he had won. He turned to Jed, his rival in more ways than one, with a sneer. Jed withered inside; he felt there was more going on than a sporting contest. Nevertheless, he did his best, which wasn't good enough. Jed toppled and lay there defeated. Tom's blood was still up; he couldn't resist one last jump. Jed was at his feet. Tom did one short, sharp jump, no hop or step, perfectly executed. He landed both feet on Jed's knee, the wooden soles of his boots splintering the bones beneath.

"That's for Sid, you bastard!"

Henry and the other boys were there in a flash and carried Tom off as fast as they could, fearing further violence. The crowd said nothing; they all knew and understood. Anyway, they recognised something in Tom that they would rather never have to face; this was someone to be friends with, especially with his family around him.

The crowds were dwindling away. It had been a reasonable fair: the family had achieved what they needed, and Tom's winnings would go into the pot.

It was always accepted that Henry would go to ale house with several friends after the fair, this being the only reward he wanted. Drinking wasn't a big thing in his life, but it had become a necessity at times. Unfortunately, a few drinks could make him unpleasant; not so much violent, but aggressive – even to his family. Occasionally heavy-handed, he never knew how frightened his family were of him – a form of alcoholic ignorance coupled with selective memory.

"Old Sam's barrow had a pig."

By 6 am the following morning, some families had long left, those being the dodgier ones, frightened that their dodgy deals would come to light and catch up with them. Others needed longer to get over the labours and excesses of the day before.

Sid and Alf had long been out and about the fields and woods in search of anything edible. Hares, rabbits and pheasants were all fair game to them, trapped, killed and left hidden, to be casually picked up later on the way past. No one brought anything back into camp for fear of being caught or questioned. A day or so before, the boys had set traps, snares and boxes. They dug feed tranches to lure pheasants into the upturned camouflaged boxes where they would stay, never attempting to go down and out. Once in the box, they would just stay there. With everything killed and hidden, the boys were back in camp and bed before the main camp stirred.

Animals fed and breakfast eaten, the Hardy family were all loaded up and on the way again to their penultimate stop, with Uxbridge as their main encampment. From there, they would travel out to various smaller fairs, still hoping for the odd last-minute deal. Again they found dealing harder with the increased competition.

Henry's mind was made up; he and the boys bought all they could as long as there was a slim profit. They all knew, without being told, that this was their last trip and where their next destination and final settling place would be. They worked slowly and quietly towards this, knowing they would sell everything and travel light for the 30 miles back to Aston and their first permanent home.

Chapter 3

The day before moving into Southall, their final destination, was the lull before the storm. Everyone was lounging around, gathering themselves for the various rigours of business and exertions of every form of entertainment and sport.

As evening came, more relaxed forms of entertainment would start. There were always willing songsters of various styles and qualities. Some would sing Romany songs, others French, Irish, Gallic or English. All songs were handed down from father to son, no one quite knowing the origins or why the particular language but obviously linked to the various family's ancestor's wanderings far and wide.

As all signs of life were dying down, people settled for sleep. Numerous scavenging dogs came visiting the camp looking hopefully for a meal, but pickings would be slim and welcomes even slimmer. The only dogs welcome in the camp were those that could provide more than they themselves needed or ate. A good rabbit, hare hunting, or racing dog was okay, but as pets, certainly not.

First light and off to Southall, the noise of which could be heard a couple of miles away. The boys knew the score as they had been told many times before. They didn't need reminding to keep all possessions together and one another inside at all times. They would have barely arrived when the first approaches began. "The early bird catches the worm" applied, with buyers preferring early deals rather than leaving it to a possible last-minute rush by too many buyers for too few horses of dubious quality. Henry had seen it all before. Others will learn the hard way, as he had years previously, and sell too quickly and cheaply, or get left at the end, unable to sell. Timing was of the essence. Henry knew what he needed and could get, and he would stick to it. A sensible deal without being greedy was his dictum - even more so this time as every-thing must go.

By midday, he had finished. Everything was sold, and a profit had been made. He might have done a little better, but things could have gone wrong; as it was, he was happy. The money was split between his and his boys' pockets which meant, for this family, "absolutely safe." Within the hour, all the family were inside the wagon. All the money was put on the table, counted and then hidden carefully away between layers of boards on the wagon floor. Spending money had been allocated - not much, but there was little to spend on outside business. The rest of the day would be for entertainment, competition and renewing acquaintances, some for the last time.

Henry had one last duty of honour to perform. Somewhere among the fancy caravans parked on the outskirts was his older brother Albert. There had been a misunderstanding over a financial deal when Albert felt that his younger brother Henry had used him in a situation to make what was considered then a large amount of money. They had disagreed. Henry did not believe he had taken advantage of his brother. Plus, on the other hand, being the oldest, Albert had received all of their father's wealth and belongings. This was quite considerable as their father had been a very successful and respected dealer.

Nevertheless, the nag was there, and Henry's sense of honour meant that now he had the money, he would dispel this in the recognised manner of disputed debts. He placed the money in a bucket, covered from prying eyes and went in search of brother Albert. His caravan with its magnificent shire horse was not hard to find, nor was Albert's portly shape sitting at the top of the steps. Henry quietly approached, placed the bucket on the bottom step, removed the cover and looked up. The brothers looked at one another completely without emotion. Not a word was spoken; there was no dislike, just an immense amount of pride and honour equally distributed and now satisfied.

Henry went back to Sara, who had now met up with some of her very few friends. There wasn't much to talk about, but Sara enjoyed and needed the rare female companionship she got.

Henry picked up the wandering little Harry, who looked like a tiny ten-year-old rather than a two-year-old: too thin and weary-looking for a baby. Although he had been ill most of his young life, he smiled at the slightest excuse or bit of attention. 'In fact,' Henry thought, 'I have never seen Harry without a smile and certainly never seen him cry.'

"Sing us a song, Jack."

The three older boys had already gone among the crowds of entertainers. Yes, they were up for being entertained, but by con men? No, they couldn't be conned; gamblers were no problem either, but girls, well, that was a different matter altogether; they held great fascination for all three. They had been warned about competing in any games or sports as this was far more serious here. After the problems Tom had got involved in, it was best just to watch this time rather than face any repercussions. Therefore, it had to be girls.

This was difficult enough as it was with the three of them, but by the time they had met up with old pals, the group was nearing ten. Being ever the thinker, Alf had pointed out that a group of ten girls was going to be hard to find, if not impossible. Nevertheless, like starving savages on a boar hunt, they were ever hopeful as well as needful. All of a sudden, like an oasis in a desert, a group of girls came into view. They were all sitting around, giggling and trying hard to look coy, posing casually while at the same time scrutinising the oncoming lambs to the slaughter. The boys might think they are lions, but they are soon to be lambs.

The ever-forward Sid, quick with an introduction, averted an otherwise embarrassing situation.

"Hello, girls. Would you all like to dance?"

Well, he was always ambitious. The observant reply came from the other team leader, Rachel, a very slim, pretty girl with long dark hair and even darker eyes that were now fully on Sid's cheeky face. He was transfixed, blown away, his confidence had gone, and he appeared to lose his hearing.

"I can't hear any music," Rachel said.

Luckily Alf still had his wits about him and came to the rescue. He produced his harmonica and began to play one of the few tunes he knew.

Also on the ball, Tom came in with, "Well, I can; can't the rest of you?" He started to jig in and out of the (by now) amused girls.

All the boys now in for a penny, in for a pound joined in, gradually followed by the girls. After all, Romany jigs didn't involve anything personal or any touching. It was fun and harmless but was the most exciting thing to happen to them in a long time. The last two to join were Sid and Rachel; both had had a sort of dumbing effect on the other, which was not in either usual character.

After a while, everyone was tired, and Alf's cheeks were aching. Things ground to stop as one after another, they fell to the ground, exhausted.

To everyone's amusement, Tom hit the nail on the head and said, "I think we started a little early. It's only mid-afternoon; we will not last the night at this rate."

On that note, they all agreed to meet up that evening at the campfire to dance and sing, as was always the custom. This little interlude made life seem great and worthwhile. All were in good spirits as they continued around the stalls and eventually back to their temporary homes.

Henry sat with Harry and Sara watching with pride as his three young men approached. He wasn't emotional, but something powerful was happening in his chest as he watched, and Sara recognised it.

That night there were revellers around several campfires with no age limit. The boys met the girls who were no longer unattended, and friendly competition between the boys was okay. All had fun. Friendships were made, and an occasional kiss was given. Gratefully received promises were made, some to be kept, some perhaps not, but that is life. Anyway, who knows who will meet again or not? Home to bed as it is soon the end of a lifestyle and the beginning of a new one.

Chapter 4

First light found most people almost silently busying themselves with packing up and heading off on their treks back to their winter quarters.

Henry and his family were quieter than most in anticipation of what Henry had decided for them. They all knew and understood, so they were willing to try and saw no point in making waves.

Albert watched from across the field as his younger brother pulled all his worldly goods from the site with just two cart horses; there were no stock animals or unsold horses in tow: he had obviously sold out. Albert, as usual, was interested but unconcerned.

It seemed to take half the time to arrive back at Aston, the inevitable always arriving quickly. They pulled up for the last night of symbolic freedom less than half an hour away from the stud and the first roofed home they would ever live in. No one said a word; everyone thought.

Morning came equally quickly, and soon they were outside the Aston estate. Henry spoke to John Burrows, collected the key, and they all went to the cottage. It was very sparse but very welcoming. The relief on Sara's face was there for all to see and more than compensated for the concern on Henry's. They wouldn't back out now, and anyway, there were a lot of pluses. The house was small, but their possessions were few making the house seem large to them. They had outbuildings, a yard, and a paddock - what more could anyone want?

Next morning first thing, Henry was at the Aston yard busying himself with all the things he saw were needed. Burrows said nothing; he knew Henry would not take kindly to too many instructions, and anyway, he was tending to the yard and horses. A number of things had been overlooked and were all of a sudden obviously in need.

'We could all learn a bit from this arrangement,' he thought.

"Best leave him alone," said the Colonel, reading Burrows' mind. "Anyway, things are getting done before I could tell him any things - just in a different order. That's what we hoped for, and now we have got it, we are struggling to get used to it. Bit of a turnaround, eh?"

The days and weeks went by. Sometimes the boys came for a day's work or two; the house became a home, and the thing they had fought against was turning out to be good.

'Home' had meant a number of different things in the past. Henry and his family were beginning to see what it meant now, and it was met with varying degrees of likes and dislikes. The older boys were used to the transient way of life, with the younger yet to be influenced, other than recognising it is a lot easier to remain in one place.

Little Harry's chances of surviving the winter were definitely improved by having a weather-proof home around him. Also, the opportunity to have her latest and what would be her last baby in a house pleased Sara no end.

When he remembered, Henry would be at work all day. It was an irregular, erratic routine which was also difficult for the Colonel. He knew it wouldn't be easy, to begin with, but he hoped Henry would get more reliable and consistent. However, once there, Henry worked among the horses: the thing he knew and loved the most. He would work without regard to time, on various stages of train-ing, breaking or ailment. As with his own, he made sure every animal was thoroughly fed and watered before he broke bread for himself.

"Feed all the animals before you feed yourself."

The older boys were much slower to be drawn into full-time employment. They were happy just to turn up for a day's work ploughing or harvesting, requesting that day's pay at the end of every day, no matter how small the sum.

The call from the old ways could no longer be resisted by Sid, who, with a fond farewell, took off with the old cart and family horse 'Mayfly,' also happy to hit the open road again. Sid had little to barter with but would find a way. He had his wits about him; he had been taught survival skills all his life, but he intended to do more than just survive. Sid thought freedom was most important, and he wanted to return to the old life - the one he knew and understood. It didn't take him long to get into the swing of things, and with the knowledge that the rest of them were settled and content, he only had himself to worry about. He could take a few knocks if there were to be some.

His first port of call was a horse fair just 20 miles away, which meant a day's steady pull for a horse and cart. He was welcomed back into the fold, helping a friend or two with tricky sales. He gambled a bit on the spot and came away a little richer. Plus, he pretended to buy a horse from a friend to keep would-be customers' attention and, hopefully, sell on again by the end of the day for profit.

Come 7 o'clock, a man sidled up and made an offer resulting in profit for the horse he thought Sid had bought earlier that day. Sid pretended reluctance but agreed to the sale and hurried back to his pal with the good news and half the profit. He had done a couple of similar deals, much to the delight of his old mate. A few more fairs like that, and he would be able to go out on his own.

That's what duly happened; he bought some good horses, some made to look lame, and some sick to be brought back to health by hook or by crook. He soon had half a dozen to work on. He would get them fit and well, and if not, they would at least look okay, well enough to sell anyway. Sid had seen his uncle Albert at various fairs. They hadn't spoken, but there was already respect there. When he went home that Christmas, he never mentioned it to his dad, Henry. There was no need for his dad to know, and anyway, he was his own man now, and his dad would accept anything without question.

Sid left home in the spring to follow the fairs. Though they were getting smaller, he was doing okay. When he reached the final fair at Southall, far from being smaller, it had grown much larger.

He stood staring across a mass of horses, ponies and people; in the middle of that hubbub, his eyes inevitably fell upon the one thing they longed to see. Someone was staring intently and unbelievingly back. Yes, it was Rachel, the dancing girl he had been so smitten with those years before. There was no stopping them; they pushed and barged towards one another. No one seemed to mind being pushed, and the crowd began to divide to let them through, sensing something important was happening. Finally standing face to face, he wrapped his strong arms around, and her she was off her feet, not that either knew.

Both, as if with one voice, said, "I thought I would never see you again."

Her family stood open-mouthed. It was too late to complain – if they had a complaint, that is. This was something no one could do anything about, and the nearest part of the crowd were cheering at them to get on and be happy.

They had only met once previously, yet all this emotion came flooding out.

Rachel spoke again. "I waited and hoped. I needed no one but you to come back."

Speechless, Sid realised he hadn't so much as looked at other girls, and now he knew why. They hugged and jigged.

Her brothers and friends stood in silent shock until Ben, the oldest, said in a loud, commanding voice, "I don't think anyone or anything should get in the way of that."

Permission had been given and gratefully received. He put his arms around his brother's shoulders and said, "Back to business." That was his consenting and leaving her to her own will.

Sid and Rachel were soon married and settled down with a child. It was good for Henry and Sara to have a grandchild for what would be the last couple of years of their lives.

Chapter 5

The Boer War came and went, leaving the family still intact, and then the First World War. By then, they had become comfortable; they had a small house with some land and managed to buy and sell from home, not having to travel much more. The horse fairs were gradually finishing, and by the Second World War, they had ended - just auctions on the major sites remained. The old lifestyle was gone. Those who survived the wars changed from horse to fun fairs. They had always been there, in a small way, but had now totally taken over. They didn't suit Sid; the wanderer was still in him. Not long after the war, he and his family emigrated to Australia, and you can't travel much further than that.

"How many beans make five?"

At five years old, Harry was frail and already weather-beaten, having only known the open road for all his young life. He was having to come to terms with the good and bad all in one go: school, learning, restrictions, close community, life along with the benefits of a roof over his head, stability, almost regular meals and possibly a future.

Labelling came early to him. "Doubt he will live long," "Won't ever learn anything," "Probably won't have long to try," "Still go through the motions of school etc."

Despite all this, Harry was a survivor. He handled everything with a smile, including the roughest of rough and tumbles, learning without trying that there would always be more than one way to skin a cat. Problems were there – always had been and always would be – not to be avoided, just normal objects to overcome and, in due course, they would be. The confidence of youth would grow and last him all his life. He was the smallest in the school but more than looked after himself with or without the assistance of his three older, larger brothers, not to mention Ruth, his sister, with her dark, Romany complexion gathering attractiveness. Hers was a power rather than strength. Even at that age, the older children, especially boys, stood back in bemused awe. Some people have it; others don't - a presence that needs no explanation; there is always something there justifiably creating it.

Ruth was enjoying the learning thing and therefore making great strides, whereas the brothers were finding it harder to come to terms with rules and restrictions. Their lives hadn't been so different. Why, all of a sudden, was it punishable to be as they had always been before without complaint? They just wanted to be free; luckily, they were too old for school. That would have been one restriction too many.

The need to work and be gainfully employed had come to his boys, but of course, it was not harder than anything else. It was regularity that was proving a big restriction.

A few years later, Harry was looking out of the junior school window at freedom. He was thinking, 'What is learning? Surely it's something you do as you go along by experiences, not by forcing you to remember things so obviously not worth remembering. No one in the school mentions how, when or what to feed animals, or how to treat their ailment, let alone breaking or training horses, how to cut wood, or provide for your family, so nothing that seems directly helpful in any way.'

Harry was sure he had learnt everything necessary: how to reap and sow, feed and water, trap fish or snare food. He had always been able to stand in any field and know without actually seeing what was there, what had been, and what would be likely. The smallest sign was enough, plus he had an unexplained sense in all types of circumstances. The awareness of possible danger was always going to be an asset. His one overriding characteristic was that anything that needed to be done had to be done and done quickly. He was happiest at full pace, regardless of the job or the reward.

Harry would get up in the morning and go out to the animals before his own breakfast, with his father's words ringing in his ears. "Never be mean to land or beast," and "Never eat yourself until your animals have eaten. They can't get their own food; you can. The land is the same; if you neglect them, it will cost five times more to get it right and healthy again than if you treated them well all the time." Animals and their welfare were to play a part in all of Harry's life.

"Don't be mean to animals or land, or they will both be mean to you."

School finished for the day. The door opened, and children spilt out as fast as the opening would allow, off in all directions to their respective homes and chores. This, although freedom, was not exactly free time. Doing chores without being nailed to a chair was a good start. Being in the open without constant instructions and demand for concentration was better, but being allowed to think for himself about whatever he wanted was the best: freedom of mind.

Of all things, food was the least on his mind. He wasn't used to much anyway, so expectancy was low; nevertheless, one way or the other, his mother Sara would have something ready at meal times.

The typical walk home would involve keeping an eye out for rabbits, pheasants, partridges, etc. and possible catching places, then collecting ears of corn to aid their trapping, the first possibility being a rabbit. By 4 o'clock in the afternoon, rabbits will all have come out of their warrens to sleep in the grass. The chances with stealth and a stick were good, but even better with a net. He would place the net in a secluded area away from prying eyes. Of course, this was poaching, which was very punishable even though it was fair game in most people's eyes. There was no rabbit today but evidence of pheasant by the small plantation of fir trees.

After a quick look around, Harry remembered seeing an old box that morning not far away. He collected it and took it back to the fir trees. He found a gully some six feet long, wide and deep enough for a pheasant to pass along. Harry turned the box upside down and placed it over the end of the gully. He got to work, blocking off any exit at the end of the box. He took the corn from the ears he had gathered and trickled them into the gully ending with most under the box. Harry knew a pheasant would eagerly eat the corn following the trail and into the box. Once inside, it would go up to try to get out. Instead of finding an exit, it would be on the gully top and still under the box, where it would stay, never trying to go down to get out.

Harry would be back later with a loop on a stick covering all options. At dusk, if the cock bird wasn't trapped, it would make the usual cackle noise giving its location away and fly up into one of the fir trees to roost for the night. The hen bird would stay on the ground, so hopefully, it would be her in the box. The stick with the loop was necessary to catch the sleeping cock bird in the tree to pull it down. It would duly have its neck rung. All eventualities covered, it was time to head off to more immediate tasks and tea.

One hundred yards later, his brother Tom was coming towards him on their latest young horse. This training might look and be fun, but nonetheless, it was important for the family's finances; a constant stream of horses schooled and ready for sale was the aim.

"Harry, did you-?" Tom started to say.

"Yes," was the instant reply, without needing to hear the whole question.

"Have you-?"

"Yes," interjected Harry again, "and I used that old box."

"Good boy. Jump up behind me, and we will go home. I knew you wouldn't miss them. I will come back later with you - we might get both."

"Are you sure we should sell this little mare, Tom? She is a good size, with plenty of bone. We could breed with her next year."

"I was thinking the same, Harry. We will have to look at the others. Dad says we will have to sell one or the others soon, and the Chapelwood fair is in three weeks, should be plenty of buyers there."

On seeing the cow standing at the gate, Harry said, "Mum hasn't milked yet this afternoon."

"No, she is poorly again."

"Right, I will jump off and do it now; the poor old girl looks uncomfortable."

"Thanks, Harry. I think you will be doing it reg-ularly from now on; Mum's arm is worse."

"Not much of a job with a good arm. I'm going to take the cob around the block. Perhaps the old man will agree to sell him instead - if I can get him a bit quieter over the next couple of weeks. His feet need trimming, and I'm not looking forward to that after last time. Still, if we start now and pick up his feet every day for the next fortnight, he should be alright in time."

By the time Harry had the cow tied up for milking, Tom had got the homemade rope bridle on the cob and was riding slowly down the road.

"I will probably meet Ruth on the way back; she should be on her way home now. I will try and get her up here as well. It could be tricky; he is only just used to one, let alone two, but it could do him good; we need to get him on fast."

"Tom, if you are not back in an hour, I will eat your dinner because you will not be needing it," Harry joked.

"Harry, even if I crawl back, I will want my dinner."

Other than the lightest of breakfasts, dinner was the only real meal of the day and, therefore, a talking point.

Harry finished milking and put the cow out and was indoors before Tom arrived back, followed by Ruth.

"Before you ask, no!" she said. "I walked back. Tom was not getting me on there, not yet anyway, or we would be halfway to Oxford by now, hanging on for dear life. Tom sees no danger whatsoever, but he will in Whichington tonight if he is there playing with fire again! Her husband is a madman. She is always black and blue; why she stays with him, I don't know. I know Tom is fond of her, but he needs to keep well out of it."

"Well out of what?" asked their mother, Sara, entering unexpectedly.

"Nothing, Mum; just joking," Ruth replied innocently.

The door opened again, and in strode lord and master Henry. A presence twice the size of his title of father, he didn't say much, as usual, and looked round at them all with a superior but approving air. From this single action, they all knew they had been acknowledged and appreciated. If there had been any problem at all, it would have been mentioned, but no, the whole family machine was functioning well.

They all ate without speaking; this done, all thanked Sara for their food in turn.

"When are Sid and Alf back?" Henry inquired of Sara, the machine's hub and memory point

"Sid's back for a while after Chapelwood fair for a week or so, then he is off to Uxbridge and Southall."

Sid had returned successfully to the old horse trading and dealing life. That was all he had ever known; he just hadn't settled to live in the one place.

"Alf won't be back for another month or so," she continued, "as he is hauling logs to Ports Mouth. I doubt if he is halfway there yet; it's a slow old drag with a load like that. Then he has got to find his buyer, and you know him, he will hang out for a good price no matter what."

Alf was another one happier on the road, well, on the move, out and about at least; these were the two older boys they were so used to it.

"Ready, Harry?" asked Tom. "Let's see what you have caught."

Harry picked up his loop stick and sack, and they were off.

"Be careful," Sara said as the door closed.

To be careful was second nature to these boys. They walked swiftly and silently, carefully observing every bush, tree, crook or cranny on either side of the lane. They walked straight past the ditch and box carried on for at least two hundred yards before circling back, one boy going left, one boy right of the lane through the trees. Eventually, they stopped thirty yards short of their final destination, sat and waited. It was dusk, so any cock bird would soon be going noisily up to his roost.

They didn't have to wait long; with the usual cluck, cluck, clucking, not one but two cock birds went up to roost. Now it was definitely worth the half-hour wait. One of these birds was going to be caught - another half an hour or so, and they would be sleeping on the branches just to wake up having been caught on the loop of Harry's stick.

Tom had already chosen which bird: the one in an ideal position, not too high, and with not too many branches around it, in other words, easy access. Not long after, Tom's foot was on a lower branch. He reached up, looped the bird and pulled the string. Caught fast, the bird was yanked down, and its neck was rung before it could make too much noise. Inevitably it made some, so more care and watchfulness would be necessary. The bird going into the sack was Harry's signal, and he was off to his box, arm and hand groping around in the box. His young but expert hands trapped the occupant, dispatched it the same way and put it into the sack.

Tom was by Harry's side. "Just one?" Tom asked.

"Yes," said Harry.

Tom was off fast, the sack in hand. Two hundred yards later, still in the trees, he hid the sack and contents. He emerged onto the lane empty-handed to meet Harry. "I moved the box over the other side of the lane; it's more innocent over there if anyone sees it."

The boys walked towards the village, away from home, once again checking there was no one around to see or catch them. This done, they turn around to go home, with Tom first and Harry a couple of minutes behind. His job was to be rear look out for Tom's safety, whose job it was to collect the sack and get home without being seen.

When Harry arrived, Tom was home, having already hung the birds in the rear pantry and was on his way to the sink for a wash. He had his assignation with Mary in Whichington. Her violent husband would soon be well and truly drunk as usual and oblivious to the brief times of happiness and pleasure his downtrodden wife and Tom were having. Tom was no drinker; to him, drinking was just a waste of very hard-earned money.

Harry and Ruth looked knowingly at each other as Tom left the house, but Sara and Henry were unaware of their son's activities and possible dangers.

Nights were drawing in, and the little oil lamp was lit, giving just enough light to allow companionship and conversation, not that Henry had a lot to say. In another hour, he would be out checking on the animals with his constant companion Harry at his side, chatting away to his mostly silent but appreciative dad.

All is well. That just left the ten minutes or so looking at the moon, again in silent thought, then inside and to bed; no point in wasting oil on the lamp. A good rest was more important.

Tom arrived home before midnight, mission accomplished. However, he was very thoughtful. He was more personally involved than he had admitted even to himself, so now he was having to think, 'What should I do? What can I do?' He was sure they were meant to be together, and they had spent the evening expressing this to one another. Until this problem was solved, it was doubtful either of them could enjoy the flippant temporary pleasure they had had. It was now far too deep for that.

Tom didn't sleep much, tossing and turning in thought. He was up even before his early-rising father, but Harry only needed one call, and he was also out helping the other two. The milking, feeding, pegging out the horses to graze, chopping and sawing were done before breakfast. They covered all the necessary outdoor and heavy work to save their ever-willing mother, not that she took any easy route. She lit the fires, heated the water, made the beds, cleaned the house and made breakfast at the perfect time for the three males and Ruth to eat and wash.

By 7 o'clock, Henry and Tom were off to work on the estate. It was now known as the stud farm because of the increased amount of horse production and activities happening since Henry had started there. Harry and Ruth were soon off to school, one more eager than the other; they were finding their own paths, after all. Ruth was clever, Harry less so and too distracted. Tom worked mornings at the stud farm with his dad, then spent afternoons at home with their own smaller horse enterprise. Soon, like the two older boys, he would branch out into his own business. It would inevitably be something to do with horses or timber or both. His brother Alf had already talked to him as he was keen for Tom to join him. It seemed the obvious choice. Tom would fell timber in readiness for Alf to cut it into planks to deliver and sell. This would cut out having to pay higher prices to outsiders for their already felled timber. Then he would give Tom the waste to make firewood from, which he could sell locally. This would work well as Tom wanted to stay here to see Mary.

Chapter 6

{Tom}

Life and the Hardy family were jogging along without too much drama for the next couple of months.

Then Tom made his break from employment, albeit only half-employed, but he was finding a comfortable income from cutting and selling firewood enough for his pleasures: a drink or two, a song or two and a woman or two.

He had access to all the wood he could sell through his brother, Alf. Once Alf had cut the main trunks out, ready to sell for planking, there was a lot of excess (all the tree tops and waste) going spare for Tom to use.

Tom worked hard and played hard; he sold and delivered his wood all over the place. He even appeared to be delivering where he hadn't sold or never would, but that's another story. Payments came in all fashions, and Tom was always happy to negotiate and accept just about anything. The ladies loved him, the husbands didn't, but proof against a wily devil like Tom was hard to find.

Although sexually driven, he really liked and respected the ladies.

There was one more than the others he had a deep feeling for; he knew she felt the same, readily accepting his friendship. The problem was a big one: she was married and obviously the faithful type. , Despite all the dangers, Tom found himself more and more drawn to her. Her husband was a brute of a man who drank profusely and showed no respect for man nor beast and certainly none for his wife. She often appeared with cuts and bruises, which seemed to be getting worse.

One day, her screams were heard and had been the talk of the area. The husband, Ben, was drinking heavily in the pub that night as usual. He was approached by a concerned man who inquired about his wife's health.

"None of your business. She is my wife, not yours," he replied.

The man was expecting to be backed up; there were plenty of others in the bar that should have also shown concern.

Someone else under the same impression said, "I wouldn't treat my dog like that."

He was immediately battered to the ground and kicked repeatedly. Did help or backup come? No!

"She is my wife, and I will do what I want!" Ben yelled. He barged out of the door to be confronted by Tom, who heard the commotion as he arrived at the pub.

"Who is going to stop me?" Ben questioned.

"Me," said Tom.

Ben swung his fist, but Tom was ready; he had been for weeks. He moved to one side and hit Ben on the side of his jaw. Tom was ready for anything, however long it took. He knew these people; he knew himself. No matter what Ben thought he had in his favour, it was not going to be enough. Before he could recover, Tom had hit him again, and the contest was over.

Ben fell in a heap, unfortunately smashing his head onto the cobbles. His skull split, and he died in a pool of blood. This was exactly what Tom's family had feared.

Tom handed himself over to the police, claiming self-defence and an accident. It was to take months, but with so many witnesses, public knowledge and opinion, plus the backing of Lord Meadows, a local landowner, employer of Tom and magistrate, the coroner recorded an accidental death.

The womanising stopped. His mind was continually on Mary; her well-being and happiness were all that mattered to Tom. It took time for her to realise it was true as his reputation had been so otherwise, but the proof was there to see. It was a year now since the unfortunate event, and there had been no philandering, just kindness and friendship for her.

All that had happened, plus his immense feelings for Mary, had changed Tom completely; they were married and, within months, had become Mormons. Tom had had no thoughts of religion before but was now completely happy. They lived in three converted railway carriages on land of their own that served as a good wood yard - just right for business. They changed their name to Smith as a sign of a new beginning. Over the years, they had five sons and numerous grandchildren. Tom and Mary lived into their 80s and died within a month of each other. They had truly found the love of their lives and couldn't live without being together.

{Alf}
Alf's intended path was a little longer. At odd times, he had worked tree felling in the large Beach woods of Lord Meadows in Oxford and Buckinghamshire. He had noticed where most of the timber was going, taking note of the apparent

wealth of the hauliers and ever-increasing demand for wood. It would take time to afford a team of horses, a timber bob trailer and equipment, let alone two teams of horses that would be needed for the long journeys, some well over one hundred miles. Therefore, he would work harder and longer, keeping quiet until his goals could be achieved.

The winters were long and hard, but they were used to worse. The family were well and beavered away while others hid indoors by the fires that were kept burning by Alf and Tom and their wood deliveries.

Spring came. Sara and Henry started gardening in earnest, something again new to them, but the ability to grow food was such a welcome thing - a new skill and interest. Life was getting fuller. Henry's iron hand had disappeared, and a more patient, compassionate man had arrived, despite the proximity of the pub and bouts of alcoholic intake.

By the time the end of spring arrived, Elizabeth/ Lizzy was old enough for school. The physical abuse from his old lifestyle and alcohol took its toll on Henry, and he fell ill and died of pneumonia. Sara wasted away, lost without him and died soon after. The couple had at least made the break from the old life and laid the foundations over the last five years for better, more stable lives for their children. The only real downside was that Ruth, who had the education and intelligence, was to waste all she had to follow her mother's path, looking after Lizzy and the boys. Luckily, all the boys were now working and mostly able to look after themselves, but a home still had to be provided. Possible suitors for Ruth were obviously going to diminish, what with her position, and they would be taking on Lizzy as well. As luck would have it, the one man left was probably the best: the local blacksmith - a friend of the family, strong in will and quiet in nature.

Chapter 7

{Ruth}

Having been that much younger, Ruth had to experience school and "book learning," etc. It was all rather alien at first, but since finding she could learn, she had thrown herself into it and her new talents and revelled in them. Soon, she was not content unless she was at the top of the class. There seemed to be no local resentment, partly because of Ruth's three elder brothers, who were rugged, to say the least. Also, partly her slim, dark Gypsy looks and attractiveness, not commonly seen in these parts, had not gone unnoticed by men of all ages. This could potentially be a problem, but for now, with such a close-knit family of a hardened nature, admirers restricted themselves to the odd furtive look. It would be a few years before any advance could be safely made. This was a girl who had learnt a lot and, above all, felt special; she was not likely to settle for second best.

Christmas came, and Ruth learned from school and local chatter what it meant. They had their first-ever Christmas dinner and celebration together as other families. It was simple but would be remembered. Sid was home on one of his frequent visits, bringing with him half a dozen horses of varying qualities.

Proud father and brothers inspected every inch of them, commenting and advising. It was all second nature stuff, but everyone avoided the obvious question, "How had he come by them?" hoping the answer was legal. He was in no hurry to move on, so presumably, all was well and above board.

This small house, sheds and fields had become a family fortress and expanding empire, a little hive of industry. January brought the new year and a new baby - an unusually bouncing baby, "Lizzy." She was born chubby and healthy, and that was how her mother was going to keep her!

When Lizzy was four, having had those few years being brought up by her mother and father, she lost them. It was not totally unexpected, but it changed Ruth's life overnight. She was now having to be a mother to Lizzy and a housekeeper for the rest. Her ever-present admirer, James the blacksmith, was still, if not more so, in awe of her. He finally plucked up the courage to clumsily declare his love for her and his will to demolish anyone or anything that would ever upset or harm her. He had become so over-the-top and enthusiastic, having held it all in check inside himself for so long, boldly demonstrating for all to see! She had to stop him!

"Half that will do," Ruth said. "I have long since fallen for you. Come for tea; my brothers will be pleased to see you as they had been expecting it."

With that, he scooped up little Lizzy and danced around the village pump with her, making it clear that she would be a welcome part of the deal.

The one dark cloud on the horizon was the house - their home. Now that Henry and Sara had gone, the family could only hope to come to an arrangement with the Colonel. Luckily, Harry was employed by the estate and was proving his worth with the horses as his father had done. Harry was keen to fix a rent to ensure a stable home whilst not being tied to working on the estate forever to keep it.

Once more, the Colonel, a very reasonable man, agreed. It was probably the best all-round; this was a family of its word that would not be pushed into a corner. They would move on; the trust would be broken. No! In the long run, a happy tenant was better than ten unhappy ones, and the rent would be paid. This family always paid back good deeds with good deeds religiously.

Life settled down again. Ruth and James were soon to be married at the heart of the family and would stay in the house and provide stability.

Two years later, all four boys had achieved what they needed enough to finance their own business needs and follow their own paths.

Ruth and James, the rock-steady hub of the family, were secure as any blacksmith-come-farrier could be in that day and age. They had three children, and they would often sit together in the evening. Out of the corner of her eye, Ruth could see James just looking at her. Sometimes he had a little tear in his eyes, quickly wiped away, of course: he adored her. He possessed all that strength, that wonderful physical fitness, those handsome looks, not to mention being the most attentive of lovers. Yet his weakness was that he could not believe his good fortune; he felt he didn't deserve her. James needn't have worried; he was everything to her. What a great feeling she got in the knowledge that wherever she was, she could feel him looking at her, his eyes saying, "I love her."

The children were bright and successful, which is what happens when from a happy home like theirs. Ruth and James lived out their lives there, with James as a blacksmith. They were the last ones to live in the house under the hill, which is sadly now in ruin.

Alf was at home when Henry and Sara died. He had taken over the head of the household as the father figure. He had achieved his goals as he always would. A very resolute strong-minded man, he had bought his horses and timber bob. He was hauling wood in all directions but had so far restricted his distance to forty miles or so. However, now Ruth and James were taking over the house and his role, it freed him up to earn larger sums by delivering logs to the coastal ports of Portsmouth and Southampton. There was still a huge amount of timber needed in shipbuilding.

Off he would go, one team pulling with the other tethered behind, walking but resting, awaiting their turn. Some hills were too steep for one team, so both would be needed. Then, on the downhill, huge wooden brakes would be used with the second team hitched to the rear to hold back the load, extra precaution being wise.

Alf earned and deserved every penny, and the cautious thinker never took a chance with his animals. One hundred miles there, one hundred miles back, it would take a month or so each round trip carrying what couldn't be bought on the way - horse feed, etc. He became quite wealthy, so he stopped the haulage and sold the horses to Harry along with the bob, who took over the dangerous arduous job. Alf was now buying and selling woodlands felling as required, which also helped Harry. Due to his illness, Harry had never walked that well and was incredible flat-footed. This made his task much harder as he would not add his weight to the load already being pulled. He walked the majority of the way there but had a ride back.

Alf had not had much time for romance, but nevertheless married later in life. He had no children, and after World War II, he and his wife emigrated to Australia and joined his brother Sid and his family.

{Harry}
"Harry's rendition of Old Man River, he just keeps rolling along."

Harry started his working life alone with his dad Henry on the Ashton estate. Henry saw his youngest son Harry in a new light without his brothers around to overshadow him. Harry was small but was, in fact, as tough and dark as teak with wiry strength. He was able to work most people to a standstill. The Colonel was pleased with him and readily agreed to rent the cottage to him when

Henry and Sara died, mainly to keep Harry around. Like his dad, Harry had not just been a labourer, but he saw the unexpected. They kept the horses sound by nipping problems in the bud, and everything was up to the mark when they were around. Anything broken was immediately mended; nothing was left for another day. Harry's only problem was he had only one speed, which was top speed. He was full bore all the time and did everything at a run. He just wanted to get on and would never give up.

He was good-looking, charming and had an eye for the girls, well, one girl in particular; Maude, one of two daughters from a wealthy family living in the next village. Maude was bright and bold but very aware of her attractiveness to men; she led Harry and others on a merry dance. He had become involved and failed to notice her younger sister. It was Maude who was on his mind when he was hauling the timber to the coast, and her he wanted to get back to.

There would be an interruption to his life; the Boer in South Africa had flared up again. After a year, it was thought Britain had quelled any problems, but it had flared up again more seriously. Harry fell into the age bracket and was called on to fight for queen and country; Victoria was ageing now but still on the throne.

An excited Harry had been given the appropriate propaganda of adventure, all finished within a couple of months, and he was raring to go. The powers that be passed him as medically fit, despite his flat feet; even marching would be difficult, and he would stand out like a sore thumb. Nevertheless, off he went only to find very little excitement but a tremendous amount of marching with the occasional bouts of trying to kill people: just the ugliness of war that went on for three years. On the other hand, he was one of the lucky ones. He not only came home, but he came home in one piece, back to the haulage, which didn't seem half as bad this time around after South Africa.

In the meantime, Maude had married Jim, a wealthy timber merchant. She had shown no loyalty and even now was being unfaithful as ever. Jim knew of her dalliances and could take no more; she wasn't the sort of person you could reason with. Jim had very low moments; very little was needed to spark off a depression. On this particular day, he had listened to Maude and her lame excuses for suddenly needing to be away for the day. He read correctly between the lines and walked blindly off to the railway track. He threw himself under the first train to come along. Just a mess was left with no signs of life; Jim had finally done what many had thought he would.

Maude was inwardly shocked on her arrival back home. He had died as she was deceiving him. Only someone as hard as Maude would take that in her stride, but that's what she did. She stayed with her two sons and carried on. She didn't feel the need to move away and start again; it was just business as usual. She never left, and at the ripe old age of ninety-five, she died there.

Harry had seen the light. It had more effect on him than Maude, even though it was not him that was with her. It was a couple of years before he became romantically involved. Even that was not easy because the one person he had real, genuine feelings for, in fact, had fallen in love with, was Maude's younger sister, Dora. She was a completely different type of girl: very quiet, pretty and with long hair she could sit on. She had watched Maude and cringed at the damage her sister had continually done. This had made her even more cautious, and she had not entered into any relationship whatsoever, but she felt drawn to Harry. This would take time, if at all, to succeed.

The bits of knowledge Dora had of her sister Maude and Harry, who she had fallen for, were proving a problem. They may have been sisters, but there were no similarities, and the differences between them were vast. Dora, the younger sister, felt overshadowed by Maude, which, under the circumstances, was only to be expected. Most things could be accepted, but the problems Dora had were different. She didn't know and would probably rather never know how much of a relationship Harry had with Maude and if it could be forgotten in the future. Would it disappear or get worse? Only time would tell.

When Harry finally proposed, Dora was ready; it was what she wanted, and she would just have to try.

Most of the area was owned by three estates. The Ayres estate consisted of a good two hundred properties and thirty-five farms, all being sold by auction. Harry and Dora went to the auction to buy their future home. There were three farms of the appropriate size, and they had their preferences, but if necessary, they would settle for any at the right price. As luck would have it, the first that they bid on, they bought. It was a bit hilly but very farmable. They were happy the last part of the puzzle was in place; they could now be married and not need anyone or anything else. With two hundred acres of mostly arable land and a comfortable house, they felt they had everything, even more so as the first of five daughters came along. Harry was still doing his timber haulage, a job to give up, but that had made it all possible. However, the farm was taking up more time, and he was not happy to be parted from his adorable wife, and she was becoming more unhappy to be left.

A life together was what they had always talked about so the decision was made: the farm and togetherness it would be. There had to be certain times apart due to the farm; after all, the horses were still the main form of transport in London. For a few years, Harry took his hay and animal fodder crops to the highest bidder. Therefore, delivery to London had to be done, mainly at harvest time and other times now and then. Harry got around the problem by being loaded and on the road by 6 am, into London by mid-afternoon, sold and delivered to be able to be back home by 6 am the next day.

"To plough with a horse 1 acre a day, walk 10 miles and 10 hours."

All went well until 1914, when the First World War broke out. Ordinary folk were unaware of the whys and wherefores, and they mattered not. Duty was calling, and there was an automatic desire for Harry to join up to fight for king and country again. However, Harry was nearly 40; his age was against him, and his fallen arches and flat feet were also an obvious problem. He failed this medical, despite trying again and again with different services and at different regiments. He failed every attempt due to the same old thing, but he had battled his war in South Africa against the Boers, so there was no dishonour. It was also pointed out that food production was of equal importance, so he fought his war from the farm with Dora and his girls.

PART 2

Chapter 8

Fred was finding it easy to doubt himself and questioned if this was it. Was it a dream or a figment of a vivid imagination? No one will ever know for sure, but the feelings Fred had were so strong. Before he was anything - other than possibly a spirit - he believed he was given the choice to be born into this life on planet earth, with the understanding that it was now or never. The world was soon to be doomed and destroyed by uncontrollable nations and progress; the big bang would arrive within the next two hundred years.

Decision made; his time had come. The lottery of which family he would be born into was obviously pre-ordained. He would be born on 16th February 1943, in a small English country village, into the most loving, protective family: mother, father, two daughters and now a son, Fred.

His mother's parents were Harry and Dora, and his father's parents were from the farm next door, Henry and Sara. All four of his grandparents were best friends. His mother, Bella, was a very intelligent but frustrated intellect. Fred always loved her from the start, and she became his lifelong best friend. His dad, Bill, was a real gentleman but coldish - a typical Cancerian man - very stoic but unable to communicate with his son Fred.

Fred's grandfather on his dad's side of the family soon died, and Grandmother Sara moved away. They met possibly ten times in all before she died, but his mother's parents, Harry and Dora, were a significant influence in Fred's life. He saw them daily for many years and had hundreds of lovely memories.

Fred's dad was a big man. One day he was carrying buckets of water to tip into the water tank - the only water supply. It was on the path along the front of the rented bungalow that was their home. Fred ran to him and grabbed him around the lower legs, this large man that he so wanted to love him. Fred could not see all of him or his face, but he knew it was his dad. Bill pushed Fred roughly aside with a sharp rebuke; Fred was two years old. It was his first rejection and one he would always remember. Was this the start of a lifelong search for affection, acceptance and self-worth? From small acorns, mighty oaks grow. This was just one acorn of rejections, failures or disappointments that happened in the early path of Fred's life. He was on a course he was not to recognise for fifty years: a path of deceit, promiscuity, fights, failed affairs and misguided behaviour. Later he learned how wrong it was and how other people suffered because of his insecurities and low esteem. However, he was cursed with the perfect non-selective memory. He was aware of all things and the right ways to handle himself and others, but unable to do so to gain self-belief. Even knowing and understanding everything as he did, he hoped he was not blaming events wrongly. It might have always been in him, and a better Fred might have handled it differently - to everyone's advantage. We will never know, but this was Fred, and hopefully explains the decisions he made.

By the time he was two years old, he was used to gas masks, blackout curtains on the windows, soldiers in the barns at night sleeping ready to move on the next morning to their barracks, and German planes overhead on the way to bomb towns and cities further west (Coventry). Half an hour or so later, these planes would be racing back over, randomly throwing excess weight, including bombs, in an effort to lighten their planes to get back to their homes in Germany, hopefully unscathed.

On one particular day, Fred, with his parents and sisters, were collecting hazelnuts from the hedges when the sky went dark. It was September

1944, and the sky was full of planes pulling other gliders behind. There were hundreds of them, all full of soldiers on their way as part of "Operation Market Garden." This was the official name when the allies made the attacks on the bridges, later to be known as Arnhem. 'A Bridge Too Far' was the name of the film they later made.

Fred remembered his dad picking him up and saying to his mother, "Something terrible must be happening. Let's go home quickly."

Although feeling largely ignored, unwanted and not good enough by his dad, he did have that much-needed male influence in his life. This came via his Granddad Harry who farmed all the land around where they lived, mainly with horses. This sparked a lifelong interest in Fred and a need to own horses.

Inevitably, the need for machinery and some modernisation had led to his granddad buying two Fordson standard tractors. For a long time, he refused to drive either of them and relied on Fred's dad, Bill, to do all the tractor work when he got home from work. The obvious eventually happened. One day, Bill was not available, and the tractor was very needed, so Granddad Harry had to drive. At this stage, this man was Fred's hero! He only had one speed; whatever he did was at full speed, hel-ter-skelter, and today was to be no different.

With his beret (which he always wore) tightly on his head, Harry swung the starting handle. This was a little man with immense strength. The tractor started, so Granddad Harry ran around and jumped on. He sat firmly, gripped the steering wheel and, with determination, he yanked the hand throttle control fully out. The beast roared; Harry lifted his foot off the clutch, and the ensemble bolted out of the shed like a racehorse from the stalls. The rear wheels were spinning, and clumps of dirt flew up behind from the metal spikes called spuds on the large, flat metal wheels. Luckily, it was in forward gear, and the field was large enough for him to have room for several laps without damaging anything or running out of space, allowing him to complete this learning curve. Half an hour later, he practised his stop, start and reverse; the engine, of course, still roaring madly. He backed the beast back into its shed and stopped, to Fred's surprise, without crashing out of the back of the shed: mission accomplished.

From that day on, you couldn't get him off the tractors; he was hooked. You could even say he had become a petrol/paraffin head.

Harry and the tractor ended back in the shed without serious incident, almost on the exact spot it had started. Harry emerged from the shed with a look on his face that Fred had not seen before.

Calmly, he said, "Well, boy, that's the future," and it certainly was.

From then, it would be difficult to keep him off this racing machine. He never did get the hang of varying the throttle; perhaps he never saw any need to: forward, back, ploughing, harvesting or whatever - full speed ahead and always with a look of total control.

Fred loved that man and his grandma, too; they also loved one another so much all their days. Fred saw it and badly wanted the same for himself. No matter what happened in the future, that was his ideal.

Harry was an Aquarius, the same as Fred, and the affinity was obvious. They were up for any-thing, imaginative, met fire with fire, extroverted, adventurous, and easily distracted. They showed a large element of 'needs must' in all actions and had a rule of never stepping back.

Fred went everywhere with him if possible.

Fred would first ask, "Can I come, Granddad?"

His reply would be, "Have you got everything?"

"Yes," Fred would reply - everything being the three things he needed to show Harry: a piece of string, a penknife to cut the string and a shilling in case Harry needed a pint of beer. Thinking back, Fred never did spend that shilling but always had it ready as promised.

"Don't tell your father."

Tractor work on that bank at Chiltern Hills farm was tricky at the best of times, so the spiked wheels were on permanently to ensure starting and stopping under any circumstances. Large trailers were in constant use, connected behind the tractor with a large metal pin that should have had holes in the lower so a safety chain could be fastened through the holes. On two occasions, Fred was in the trailer behind the tractor being driven uphill by racing granddad when the pin jumped out of the trailer. Now free, the trailer and Fred sped backwards down the hill, ending up in the hedge. Luckily, Fred and the trailer were unharmed. Harry turned the tractor around and came down the hill to pull them out of the hedge. He reconnected the trailer, this time with a safety chain through the holes.

On both occasions, Harry's words were, "Don't tell your father."

Fred's father was safety conscious, whereas Harry never recognised any danger.

"Tea in a saucer with butter on."

Harvest time came, and the first job was to cut, by hand, a path for the tractor all around the fields so as not to damage any crops. Granddad Harry was with his scythe at the front cutting the corn; May, Fred's aunt, his mother's younger sister was next. She had a ripping hook, tidying up and laying the corn in groups for Fred to follow behind. He was making straw bands to tie around and make sheaves, then putting them on the hedge out of the way as they went.

To Fred, farming was sore arms from standing sheaves of corn up into stooks, hundreds of harvest bugs bites on his legs, a back burned by the sun, fingers frostbitten in the winter while topping and tailing turnips, face cut and swiped while cutting hedges, and fingers bleeding from stone picking a large number of Flintstones on this hills. However, these were all minor details when accompanying Harry. All these things were pleasantly punctuated by his grandma bringing out food and warm tea for a daily working picnic or two. It was a great life - no electricity, no mains water, and five miles from a bus or a phone. There was a toilet at the end of the garden with a bucket to be emptied weekly. The family had a tin bath on a Friday, whether they needed it or not. The one lot of water used by every-one; Fred was never first in the bath.

"Harry's pit stop pony."

There were three main markets close to the family farm; High Wycombe, Reading and Thame; they all had their different stories to tell. Fred and dad Bill borrowed Granddad Harry's pony and cart to go to High Wycombe market. They fairly flew, their hair blowing in the wind, eyes streaming, faces splattered with mud, all at the pony and Harry's usual pace. They arrived safely and in good time. The chicken was sold, purchases made and loaded, sandwiches eaten, and tea drunk; they never went anywhere without Mother Bella supplying relevant sustenance. There was still time to sit and relax for a while, confident that the pony would fly home at its usual speed, and that was the way the journey started.

They flew as far as the first village, where the pony seemed to develop steering problems. No matter how they tried to keep it going straight up the road, it continually turned left and ended up in what turned out to be The Swan public house; it stopped there and refused to move. This truly was a pony of habit, habits that it had learnt from Harry and his trips to the market. Evidently, Harry regularly had a beer on the way home, and the horse felt it had to comply and waited for a beer to be drunk before moving on. At that stage, Bill was happy at the horse's antics and had a beer, but less than fifty metres away was another pub, and it stopped again. Bill, now getting the hang of things, hurried into the pub to comply!!! Only one problem - how many more pubs were there to go? The pony found it impossible to pass a pub on a homeward journey because of Harry's habits. Harry had obviously been a sociable man; they arrived home late but happy.

At home on Friday night, Harry would ask his wife Dora's permission to visit the local pub for a well-earned pint. It was all approved, but he had her words of warning ringing in his ears.

"Harry, if you are not back by 10 o'clock, the lights are going out."

The significance was that the lights at that time were oil lamps. If the lights were on, he could easily find his way home, but if the lights were out (after 10 o'clock), the darkness and influence of the beer made this difficult. It could lead to him walking miles too far, trying to find a light to guide him. On the left side of the road, theirs was the only house for three miles and easily missed. Either way, whatever happened, it was always conducted with good grace and undying love that was like a physical presence.

At Thame market, Fred was around eight or nine years old, standing by the animal pens. He watched sadly as the obviously very retarded assistant who had stopped for his break opened his packet of jam sandwiches. Unfortunately, one of the two sandwiches fell to the floor and was lost. His loss upset Fred badly and, even more so, the awful sense of guilt for being much more fortunate than this lad.

Moments later, an old man with the obligatory stick, hat, gaiters and smock (brown cover-all jacket) appeared at Fred's side. He was often at the market, and he said, "You are Darkies lad."

Fred said, "No, I'm not."

The old replied even more confidently before striding off, "Oh, but you are."

Fred took some time before deciding whether to mention it to his dad or not. Finally, he took the bull by the horn, grasped the nettle and with that double courage, told him.

He said, "No, they are wrong. You aren't Darkies lad. You are Darkies' grandson. They call your granddad Darkie because of his dark skin. Because you are always with him, even that brother of his thought you were his, but he guessed wrong."

Fred had finally met Harry's brother Tom, and looking at them both, it should have been obvious right down to the boots and gaiters.

Chapter 9

That name, 'Darkies lad,' would enter Fred's life thirty-odd years later when he was living in Wales and heavily involved in horses. He was at a trotting race when he saw the name of a horse called "Darkies lad." Nostalgia alone led Fred to put all the money he had in his pocket on him to win. He did, and several more times over the next ten years. He was a grade 1 trotter and became quite famous before being used as a successful stallion.

At Reading market, the auctioneers were 'Shortland and Thimbleby.' This was the big trip - the market they went to on serious business like machinery or to get better prices for bigger groups of animals.

Bill was attempting to buy a tractor. It all became serious, and an argument began with the auctioneer. He was a bit too clever and was taking imaginary bids against Bill so he would bid more, but Bill had twigged what was happening and stopped bidding. Next, the auctioneer tried to wriggle out and claim Bill had offered more than he had. Bill made him go back several bids to the last one he had legitimately made.

"Now show me who genuinely bid more," Bill demanded.

Of course, the auctioneer couldn't.

"You shot yourself in the foot, old man," Bill said. "I will pay 49 pounds or nothing. Take it or leave it."

The auctioneer said, "I can't be bothered to argue with you - have it for 49."

Still not happy with this response, Bill said, "If it is an argument, then keep it; I won't buy at any price - or anything else in future. Let that be a lesson to you." He walked off.

"A ewe's fart is worth two cow shits."

Meanwhile, Harry had hired a lorry to take fifteen bullocks to market - one-year-old fattened prime beef. They sold well, and he had also decided, against Dora's wishes, to buy a herd of sheep, so he loaded them in the lorry for the driver to make the return journey. When Harry, Bill and Fred arrived home by car, the lorry of sheep arrived, and Dora was also waiting at the roadside to discover the unknown contents.

When the lorry arrived, Dora heard a baa, baa sound.

"Harry, is that sheep?" she asked.

"Yes," he said proudly.

"They are not staying!" she said, with her heckles rising more by the moment. "They go back now. I hate those useless bloody things."

"I bought them!" he argued. "I can't send them back."

"I don't care," she replied. "They go now."

Where or how they went, nobody seemed to know, but they did. Dora had put her foot down, and Harry accepted it happily. Bill didn't have his tractor, but they all had been thoroughly entertained.

Home life had its ups and downs too - good and bad, a regrettable example of which happened at Fred's older sister's wedding - a day for family reunions. After the ceremony, the reception was underway when an unfortunate chain of events was to unfold. Enter Fred, the showman with an air gun, at the far end of the house. Across the field, you could see hens and, more importantly, a large cockerel, performing as his usual aggressive self. Carefully Fred gathered around him as many cousins as possible impressionable ones. Fred was preening, as well as Mister Cock, and he calmly announced he was going to shoot the cockerel. He was working his audience as much as he could into what he hoped to be a frenzy - a mixture of fear, anxiousness and tears.

"Oh, yes, I'm going to shoot him," he said, raising the gun.

Some children ran to tell their parents what Fred was about to do; others were pleading for the cocks life. Fred carefully aimed wide of the mark, also knowing normally he couldn't hit it if he tried, plus he didn't really want to hit it. He fired somehow, and God only knows how or why, but that underhanded cock dropped dead, shot through the head. Fred stood there in shock and disbelief. Some squealed, some cried, and some ran away, but the truth was, somehow, that fucking cockerel had bettered Fred. Fred felt the unmistakable hand of Bill on the back of his neck as he had several times before. It was bedtime for him with a sore bum again.

An hour later, he was lying in bed, feeling recovered and listening to the party. He decided not to miss anymore, so he climbed out of his bedroom window and went to the rear of the house, avoiding the general throng and Bill; he would party alone. He found crates of empty beer bottles and some with some beer in them. Now, if he tipped up enough, he could probably get merry or a bit happy. Fred was soon halfway to dizzy enjoyment when the current bottle with dregs in reached his lips. Unluckily, there was a wasp inside who objected to being disturbed, so it stung Fred inside his mouth. Fred's mouth was used to strong words, but in the soft and sensitive place of the sting, the pain was such it needed all sorts of expletives to overcome. Unfortunately the severity of the pain and the noise of his suffering meant he was heard throughout the place. It reached the ears of the enforcer Bill, who sadly had not yet reached that alcoholic state of happiness; he arrived being his usual punitive self. Corporally punished and back in bed under threats, Fred decided enough was enough for one day. It had not gone well, so it was time to sleep and start again in the morning.

There seemed to be some bad feelings still hanging over from that day. It came to a head a few days later with Fred using a rude word or two and taking off at a run - and run he could! Bill was a walker; with long strides, he covered the ground relentlessly. Fred had planned his escape route; he would throw the brute off track and double back under cover of the wood to a shed by the wood side. Then he would wait for the night when hopefully, all would be forgotten, and he would be welcomed home! He ran due west out of sight, turned south as planned under cover of the wood, and then due east to the shed.

'That should fool him,' he thought to himself, with the mental picture of his dad standing somewhere far behind scratching his head.

Fred left the wood and went straight into the animal shed. He laid in the long feed trough at the rear and got comfortable to wait it out. Surprisingly soon, he heard heavy footsteps; a large hand reached in and yanked Fred out of hiding, and the other hand gave Fred a clip around the ear. Fred thought his dad must have had an early form of inbuilt satellite navigation, or he wasn't human. He never loosened his grip all the way home. The satisfaction he gained by outwitting and catching Fred seemed to placate his brain as he completely forgot the sore bum bit. Instead, he put him down derisively and left Fred to beaten thoughts of uselessness.

Little did Bill know that within a month, Fred would, albeit by accident, burn his newly built wooden garage to the ground. He had borrowed a Tilly lamp full of paraffin from Wally next door, and, with his dad's permission, he was mending his motorbike in the garage at night by tilly lamp light.

Petrol accidentally splashed on the lamp, and everything went up in flames. He ran, calling his dad, who now was needed to be his saviour. Bill duly arrived and emptied the adjoining shed of dozens of bottles of homemade wine, then went back indoors to let it burn. Wally arrived from next door to inquire about the health of his lamp. He never really understood the legalities of lending dangerous equipment to a minor and just kept demanding a new one!

For all this, Fred needed to earn some money, and luckily, there was a bounty paid by pest control of one shilling for every grey squirrel tail you could produce. He had a shotgun and set about with squirrel extermination.

After years of oil lamps for light and solid fuel for cooking and heating, Bill decided Calor gas in bottles linked to the lights and cooker by tubes throughout the house was the way to go. Within a week, he had installed it all, and they were modernised.

Fred was shooting quite a lot of squirrels and had only one shot left, so he waited hidden in the wood for just one more squirrel. He waited and waited to make sure of the last shot, and then the chance came. In hopped a squirrel; Fred took careful aim and pulled the trigger, but nothing happened – it had misfired. He tried again but still no bang, so he went home, now and then aiming at something and pulling the trigger. He sat in the kitchen, aimed at the radio – nothing. He aimed at the dog, by now not thinking straight and had completely forgotten the shot left in the gun, but nothing happened. Then he aimed the gun towards the lamp. The forgotten cartridge in the gun fired; it blew the new lamp off the ceiling and made a hole in the roof, shattering bits of slate.

Fred stared up in disbelief. The damage was right next to where the scorch marks of another unfortunate incident still remained. On that occasion, when he was pretending to light a firework called an air bomb in the kitchen to frighten his sisters, the match slipped. The bomb shot up and stuck on the ceiling, where it made a defining bang, showering sparks into the box of fireworks, which all went off in seconds. Standing there reminiscing about that, and now the gunshot, with smoking gun in hand, he could hear those heavy footsteps approaching the back door that once had slammed on the cat's tail and cut it off, leaving it with balance problems. There was no time to hide; this time, he was caught red-handed as Bill's timing was once again immaculate. There was something not human about that man - some form of sixth sense similar to that possessed by our local policemen who also had the knack of appearing when least wanted. For example, the one and only time Fred was called upon to do the comparing private parts trick with two girls of similar age to him. Why was it Fred's turn to show them when Copper Cook stood up on his bicycle pedals and looked over the hedge to see everything? It was a one-in-a-million chance he would have been on that little country road at that time, and even so, a one-in-three chance it would be Fred showing and not one of the two girls. But no, it was him, and what's worse was he never got to see the girls' parts, and they had been the prime instigators.

Copper Cook could never keep his mouth shut, and all parents and probably all interested parties were informed. That night as Fred entered the kitchen, the enforcer was sitting with a shoe last on his lap, mending shoes and hammering, extending the life of their footwear. He hooked Fred on his shoulder with the hammer, pulled him back for interrogation and the ritual arse discolouration and then sent him to bed. All this was only to increase Fred's interest in sex. Bill, however, returned to nailing on another piece of wellington boot sole to the bottom of Fred's well-worn shoes. These shoes had caused Fred to slip and, not for the first time, twist his ankle.

Bill's answer to any problem was the same. "That needs white oils rubbed on it for a few days; it cures all the animals' problems."

White oils turned out to be horse liniment (it stunk); it also meant three more days in school with a very smelly leg and ribbing from the other children.

It never seemed to cure anything, but Fred had to smile and say, "Thank you, Dad."

Chapter 10

Green Remembered Woodlands

They were fortunate to experience fields of dreams, plus an authentic combination of boyhood innocence and freedom in those times.

It's 9 am, and the weekend is here. Fred pumped his bike tyres up. He had the usual things like string and a penknife in his pocket, and he pedalled off down the common hill to Town End. The journey there was all downhill and easy; therefore, the trip home was all uphill and very much slower. He would also nearly always return after dark, having spent all day between Town End and Bennett in the field of dreams, 'Barcrafts.'

Tim and Fred would walk the length of that field to meet up with Dick and Chris, the Avery boys, at their house. Their ever-patient and amiable mother said little but exuded the feeling of welcome to them all. After an hour or so of table tennis or bar billiards and, more than likely, a very welcome snack, these outdoor boys got itchy feet to seek the open air. Cricket bat, ball and wickets in hand, the next stop was Barcrafts. Although not the best-kept cricket pitch, it was certainly a popular venue and undoubtedly the field of dreams and dreams yet to be made. By now, they were joined by Warring Cowley's boys, Bert and Worzel. Soon after the first few overs were bowled, the Cowley boys were involved in verbally abusive sparring, which then turned to physical abuse. No longer just sparring, a pitched battle turned into a running battle. Bored with chasing, Worzel went home; Bert, bruised but unbowed, stayed. After all, this must be the beginning of his nickname, 'Iron hands' – catching that hard leather ball at any speed.

An hour or so later, Chris was next to leave, answering the call of the farm and the Fordson Major. It was time for him to get the cows in for milking. The call and importance of the farm were never to leave him; it was his dream that became true. After a few years of early distraction, he got his wish - he farmed in a big way very successfully.

Dick, Bert, Tim and Fred played on, happily chatting and bantering about every possible subject and dream world. Barcrafts had that effect. Cricket was occasionally abandoned temporarily while the boys indulged in climbing one of the two large trees. Both were a dream to climb and play in, just as though they had been grown specifically for them and their entertainment.

This done, eighty yards away in a corner, there was a breachable hedge leading to an orchard containing the biggest juiciest apples imaginable and cob nut trees always loaded with nuts. This can only be described again as a dream come true. Apples eaten, pockets stuffed with cob nuts, slowly back to cricket. Daylight is beginning to go, so they make good use of it.

A few more overs later, and it's still darkening.

They hear the unmistakable words, "How is the fag trade?" and "I will show you how to bowl a googly." It's Bill, Dick and Chris's dad, on his way home from the day's work on the farm, appearing out of the mist and evening light - another dream. Bill bowled his googly, smoked his fag and walked on towards his wife and dinner, smoking his cadged cigarettes (the fag trade had been good for him again).

The boys would soon part for their respective homes. Tim and Fred first walked the length of Barcrafts to Tim's home, where his mum, the unflappable Ethel, always seemed to have a smile on her face. She was a happy, sincere lady who idolised her son, Tim. Half an hour there, and then it was time for Fred's long uphill track home in the dark, leaving the field of dreams and the valley behind again.

On some weekend visits, the same groups of boys rang the church bell or had adventures with Robert the bull. It actually gored Dick's dad Bill badly, but he was rescued by his sister Doris beating Robert back with a gumboot while dragging Bill to safety.

The boys visited the church where there was a very deep well. They dropped stones into it and waited a long time before hearing a splash. Just along the road was the haunted Cross Lane pond with several sightings of ghosts and nightly sounds of horses and an old mail coach pulling hard up the hill by the pub. Living in the large house in the village was the much-fancied daughter of an important American officer, Lynn, who teased them all. The boys moved down the road to Jack and Les Stallwoods' ex-WD yard, full of ex-army vehicles and lorries. Some had bicycles packed in them and tyres - all sorts of goodies to play with. Also in the village was a girl guide camp that, for three weeks every year, supplied dozens of girls who were as eager to meet the boys as they were to meet them.

Last but not least, the boys had to take confirmation classes given to them by the reverend, Benjamin Corder, and his lovely old wife, Miss Brown. All the boys held this old couple in great respect. They were the last people imaginable that the boys would want to appear disrespectful to. However, for one annoying reason or another, they were easily made to giggle, which would turn into an awful, unstoppable, infectious impulse to laugh. They knew it was going to happen, try as they might. Despite threats of violence among them, they would do it every night after lessons. They all came out with aching stomachs and running eyes, thoroughly ashamed!!!!!!

Life took several turns for Fred, some big, some small, some upsetting, in fact, all possible things that life could throw at him. One of the main things was that Fred's mind always returned to those boyhood days and the field of dreams. After that time, Fred had a lot of friends and acquaintances, all accepted and forgotten, but not those boyhood ones; they were much more memorable. It was as though they were a dream, but not just dreams - haunting memories. They would be the ones that would have meant so much to him.

This was Fred's humble but lovely early life, so just imagine the change and surprise that was to confront him upon passing the entry exam and arriving at a very prestigious famous school with immense academic and sporting records. He found he was one of a kind; the others, upper-class privileged boys from wealthy parents or sons of officers from the military. It was very hard to understand, so Fred needed to find his own place in this society. Unfortunately, he chose the only one he really knew. He did not have the arrogant bearing or eloquent ability to argue, nor the confident attitude that the others had, so he resorted to being the tough kid on the block. Whether true or not, he could achieve it and his place in the pecking order. Sadly, he was always easily side-tracked; he had the ability, but his concentration level was low.

In the countryside where he was born and brought up, hunting for food was important, as well as being a great test of knowledge and cunning. He had been taught a bit but learned most things by experiment: success and failure. He had sat in woods near fir trees as pheasants prefer them. At dusk, the cock pheasants inevitably cocked up - that is, fly up into the branches making a clucking noise to roost for the night's sleep. This would leave the hen bird hidden on the ground, more than likely in a nest that sometimes she would fill with eggs. No one with any sense would kill the hen bird because she was the future along with her young. The cock bird is different; he would be easily replaced. Fred would wait for a while, letting him doze off, and then reach into the tree and grab him without shooting. A shot would have frightened any others and would be heard by any gamekeeper. Also, to shoot, he would have to create a distance for fear that being too close, the shot would smash the bird too much and make it useless to clean and cook.

Very soon, Fred realised he needed a shorter shotgun, so he cut the barrels of an old shotgun and cut the wooden stock. Now he had the perfect gun. The shot would spread and weaken, doing much less damage to dinner. Also, so many times while driving the lanes, he would spot a pheasant by the roadside or close anyway. Normally, he would have to stop the car, get out fast and hope it was still there. Most often, it would be gone, but now, while driving, whatever he saw, he could shoot with his sawn-off gun out of the car window.

One particular piece of woodland overlooked Grange Farm, where the owner, Mr Steel, lived. Fred would have one shot in that wood, then have to leave as he would see Steel get in his car and drive around what had to be a longish route ending up where he heard the shot; he often tried to catch Fred. Fred decided to have fun with him. He shot and saw him drive off in his car, but this time, instead of Fred driving home, he drove down towards Steel, passing him halfway in the opposite direction. Steel carried on to the wood, and Fred carried on to Steels' house. Outside the house, he shot again, making Steel turn around and drive back toward his house, passing Fred again, going in the opposite direction. Fred repeated this twice, only this time, he stopped at the passing place. He had, of course, by now hidden the gun on the way. He got out and sat on the bonnet of his car. Steel arrived, driving in a hurry, and Fred waved, challenging him. Steel slowed but now realised the truth of the situation: Fred was literally daring him to make the next move. He didn't; he went home, knowing some things are useless and can't be beaten; a great lesson for him and Fred went home as well.

Everyone in the local pub knew the score, and there was a lot of banter disguised enough to prevent a problem from developing in a personal way.

One phrase used between members of the opposition was, "We have problems with foxes."

The answer to this was, "Oh, yes! The main problem is a large white fox."

"Yes, I know the one."

Then a challenge was thrown out loud enough for Fred to hear. "That white fox won't get my pheasant - the one I have outside my bedroom window every morning."

Fred thought it best to strike while the iron was hot and decided he would nab it long before they thought he could get around to it.

At 5:30 am the very next morning, Fred parked twenty yards away, leaving the car pointing in the homeward direction, engine running. He softly walked up with his sawn-off shotgun, shot the pheasant under the man's window, took three or four steps picked it up and smartly left to the car and home. He looked back as he drove away; the bedroom light had come on, but Fred was well away, leaving only a few feathers in the garden.

Fred couldn't wait to go to the pub the next day, but the opposition didn't come for three days, probably out of embarrassment.

When they finally came, Fred greeted them with a smile and said, "How is your garden pheasant?"

They pretended not to understand, but he saw in their eyes that they knew and were extremely shocked and annoyed.

Chapter 11

Fred had been in business for a year or so, and things were going quite well. He had a little money and, in those days, no end of opportunities. At breakfast time daily and lunchtime most days, he visited the black and white cafe where Cyril had lots to offer. At the rear, there was a shed full of goods dropped off by magpie lorry drivers who were very good at misappropriating not only the goods that they carried but also fuel and spare wheels etc., of their work vehicles. Cyril was an agent for everything for everyone, including a motorcycle policeman who rejoiced in the name 'The lone ranger.' He could often be seen riding out with a box of goods, butter etc., on his handlebars.

Cyril had been very good with great tips for horse races. He was a bookies runner on the side and often told Fred the name of 'sure thing' horses, which Fred gratefully put reasonable sums of money on and always seemed to win.

One day, on the phone, Cyril said to Fred said, "Hit the beach, Fred. Hit the beach - it's a good one; big odds, twenty-to-one and a great chance. Hit the beach, hit the beach."

Fred did hit the beach. He went to the local betting shop and put one thousand pounds on Hit the Beach to win. This was the maximum bet this bookie could accept (thank goodness for that); it came nowhere!! Fred could blame no one, but from that day on, he severely limited his maximum bet. 'Once bitten, twice shy,' he kept telling himself.

In 1963, life as Fred knew it and wanted it ended - never to be the same again. There were other world-changing events, such as the assassination of John Kennedy, but the most momentous mind-destroying for Fred was after a long illness, cancer took his Granddad Harry. His dad, Bill, was with Harry when he died. Without realising it, Fred had avoided too much contact towards the end, but that was his biggest regret. However, he did manage to be there to kiss him. It was the first time he had kissed the dead, and one of his eyes had slightly opened. It had been carefully closed by Bill when he died, but as so often happens, within a day or so, one or both eyes fractionally opened. It may be fanciful thinking, but he so hoped Harry could see Fred there, late though as he was, he was where he wanted to be. Bill recounted how Harry, nearing death, imagined he was in the small wood called Pollards with Polly, the horse and cart, collecting and cutting firewood. The words he used and the involuntary movements of his body perfectly mimicked what his mind was absorbed in. He truly believed he was doing work and duties even so close to death.

A week later, the funeral cars and hearse arrived. The procession to the funeral service in Oxford began in very slow reverence - the slowest journey Harry would have ever made. No racing full-bore over hill and dale this time, Granddad.

"I hope you approve," Fred said in a low voice.

This was his last day with them, and selfishly, Fred didn't want it to end soon. The funeral train zigzagged along the country lanes from village to village. There was hardly a gateway, field or house without a respectful person or family, hats off, bowed in respect.

"Who are all these people?" Fred thought he had certainly never seen most, if any, before, but he was very grateful that they had wanted to see the old man off. Fred now realised that he had then disconnected himself from the reality of it all. How he had done it, he didn't know; it was certainly not knowingly. Perhaps it was a form of self-defence; without it, he would have been an emotional wreck. Very soon and for the next few days, the emotional protection disappeared, and he was glad it did. It was hard, but Fred wanted to rejoice in Harry's memory at will and take strength from it. *"There's worse things at sea."*

Just over a year later, Fred had a strange experience. Did it happen? Did he dream it? Was it a daydream, or was it in some form of parallel life or thought pattern? Whatever it was he was again grateful and felt honoured. In whatever state of mind he was, he found himself walking across the old farmland. There was a new, high fence dividing one field from another where he saw his Granddad Harry walking towards him.

He said, "Hello, Granddad."

Harry had on his boots, gaiters and his beret on the back of his head, exposing that balding top he had. "Hello, boy."

Fred struggled for the right thing to say but came out with, "I suppose you get a lot of time for walking now."

Harry replied without hesitation. "No, not much. We are kept busy with plenty to do; in fact, not much spare time at all."

At a loss for more words, Fred said, "It's really nice to see you, Granddad. I hope we will meet again soon." Fred thought Harry said yes and went on walking slowly.

For a long time, he never mentioned it to any-one, he just hoped he would meet him again, but he never did. Eventually, Fred mentioned it to his mother, Bella.

"Well, you are the first to meet up with him," she said as though it had been bound to happen. That made Fred even more sure he shouldn't have mentioned it because he felt he had jinxed any chance of meeting again. He had no idea if anyone else met or spoke to Harry, but if they had, Fred presumably thought they were more sensible than he had been and kept it to themselves. He would only say good luck to them; he knew how much his meeting had meant to him.

Fred had probably neglected the lovely Grandma Dora, but promised never to neglect her again from this day. She was lost without Harry, but in Fred's own grief, he had forgotten just how much more grief and sorrow were being suffered by Dora. Harry had been a figurehead. Nobody saw him upset or angry; he went through life happily, sing-ing at the slightest excuse, sometimes in French, sometimes in English, sometimes in Romany. He was always happy. No matter how things went wrong or why, his reply was always the same. "There's worse things at sea." No matter what adversities needed to be faced, that statement and his understanding of it gave Fred the ability and strength to do as Harry always did. He would smile and sing his way through, knowing there is always a good and amusing side to everything; look for it, and it will be there. In his memory, Fred would never give up; he would just smile and sing.

PART 3

Chapter 12

Fred enjoyed early school life, successfully passing the exam and achieving a place at grammar school, where he hid a lot and just aimed to get through. Being a small village country boy, he knew no better and would learn to regret it deeply. This was a God-given chance for a great education; luckily, he was bright enough to get by unnoticed. Also, sports, especially rugby, would come to his rescue, helping him to fit in and feel part of this grand establishment. He had developed other dubious talents as on cross country running days, his least-liked activity, he would run hard across the first field, then hide behind the cricket pavilion until the others completed the rest of the course. As they returned, Fred would rejoin the race not too near the front so as to avoid suspicion. He soon noticed that Roman Catholics were excused from attending morning prayers. Well, a change of religion would secure Fred an extra hour of free time every morning. Also, choosing carefully in which lesson and with which master to use his next trick, as soon as the master turned his back to write on the blackboard, Fred would put his foot on his chair and desk to jump out of the window and not be missed. Then, at a well-judged moment, he would complete the return journey, also unnoticed, much to the amusement of fellow classmates.

The last few years of school became serious. Fred had always found it necessary to be a rebel to have his own place there, but things suddenly changed. It had been normal procedure for him to fail to turn up for detention, partly because it was a long way from home - two buses and a five-mile walk. Fred preferred to be called to the headmaster's office on Monday morning to be caned - six of the best.

This week would be different; Saturday was rugby day. Although an away game this week, Fred had noticed the boss, the headmaster, in the crowd as he was an avid Welsh rugby fan. The game went okay for Fred; nevertheless, as expected, Fred was called to receive the usual punishment the following Monday morning. He waited and waited; he was obviously going to be dealt with last. His turn finally came.

"Come in," said the boss. "Sit down."

'That's unusual,' thought Fred. 'It's normally "Bend down."'

The boss continued. "I was at the match on Saturday. You had a good game; in fact, you were the only boy to get stuck in."

From then on, they talked rugby only until he finally said, "Get back to your class."

Fred looked meaningfully at him.

"No, off you go," he repeated, giving him a telling look that made it clear no further discussion was required.

From that moment on, Fred was a changed boy. He walked back feeling a good foot taller than usual - he had found his place at last. And not just found it, but he had been given it by none other than the boss. He belonged - no longer to be a rebel, now a proud, well-behaved student. He just hoped it wasn't too late. Was the boss aware of what he was doing? Was it on purpose? Who could know? One thing was certain, Fred was extremely grateful.

When the end of school finally came, Fred could not face the final goodbye prayers knowing the emotion of leaving this fabulous establishment would be too much to handle. His tough boy image would be gone, and he would cry.

With school finished, it was time for him to become the smart dresser and the girl chaser. The truth was, looking back, the picture he had in his mind was of him standing there looking "sheer class" in green bell-bottom trousers, Winklepicker shoes, and luminous yellow socks. He wore a tight, tailored Ben Sherman shirt, open at the front exposing a chain and medallion, with shoulder-length bleached hair and a pork pie hat with two feathers in the band … 'Those were the days!'

Often laying coolly on the settee with his eyes closed, taking in the strains of modern music like Paul Anka singing pleadingly, "Oh, please, stay by me, Diana." Fred was thinking sadly of his own situation with his ex, Diana, desperately trying to understand how she could possibly pass up a man of his dashing appearance as he was then. 'Her loss,' he thought. But really wanted her to be a winner, allowing him to proceed with his plan towards seduction mode; he would even keep his pork pie hat on if she preferred. What would he not do for a glimpse of those Airtex knickers he had been led to believe all girls wore with the inevitable hair or two poking through the material?

Fred's confidence had been boosted earlier on by an aunt.

On his way out, dressed to the nines, she took one look at him and said, "Someone is going to be lucky tonight."

'Yes,' thought Fred, just hoping the girls were as able to recognise the obvious and make sure they got lucky too.

Who got lucky or unlucky?? Who can tell, or who can judge? However, a year or so later, someone got pregnant, and six months later, Fred got married.

"It will never work," people said, "at 16 years old, no, never."

But for 35 years, it sort of did, and then life for Fred restarted on a whole new level. His original and most appreciated life had ended when he was 18; his grandfather Harry died, and every facet of life changed. Even with his grandmother Dora still a big part of his life, as much as he adored her, it was never the same without her husband, Harry. Almost immediately, her diabetes got worse, and five years later, gangrene in the feet led to her having both legs amputated above the knees. That amputation was bad enough, but the amputation of Harry from her was so much worse.

Misery and unhappiness set in. All her daughters except Fred's mother practically deserted her. Fred could still hear her while living with his parents as she did for her last few years, calling "May, May, May" through the hedge between his parents' house and her other daughter May's house, just hoping May would reply and at least spend some time chatting to her. She needed so little, yet May and her three other sisters did not bother; it was obviously too inconvenient. Perhaps they were worried they might have to look after her sometimes.

There were so many things and events that made the emotional Fred likely to cut loose from the family. Anyway, for many years, he was too busy; working to provide for his wife and family, which developed into needing school fees. Luckily, business got better for a few years, but school status and fees increased vastly as well. Fred worked harder and harder to maintain the standards. He had started the business on a shoestring with no capital whatsoever. Every penny earned was spoken for before being received. Bills needed to be paid in strict rotation, so anyone demanding to be paid out of turn would cause chaos. Inevitably, the appropriate phrase for what came next was "rob Peter to pay Paul," but this only works for a limited time as Peter wants to change places with Paul.

Any attempt to gain time to pay or credit from either was met with a firm "No, that would mean we would be financing your business."

'Okay,' thought Fred, 'there are other ways to go.'

Firstly, choose one and pay them and immediately run up a large month's account and change to another supplier. Next, being in the motor trade,

Fred needed to go to the car auctions and bid on and buy a car with a cheque. This gave him three days to sell it before his cheque was presented to his bank for payment. If it did not sell quickly enough, then he would visit a friendly car dealer to take out finance on it for Fred to pay, giving him more time to sell it. This also kept his credit clear at the auction by paying them with the finance company's money and making it possible to buy again. A little bit of homework in the local pubs would help the choice of the next purchase. All the time, he was hoping business would improve enough to get off this self-inflicted treadmill. For some years, it worked; obviously, it was close, and the occasional fight broke out. There was also a court case or three, but all in all, nothing Fred could not handle, and he did.

Chapter 13

All his life, Fred had lived in the country and never had neighbours. Now all of a sudden things, were going to change; his wife and four children needed a bigger house, and he could afford one. The bits of skulduggery in motor trading etc., had provided the cash, but to stay clear of the clutches of income tax, he needed a mortgage or mister tax man would be asking where this cash came from. A visit to his shady accountant was called for, and Fred could see no problem, but there was one.

The jealous accountant started off by saying, "My son can't get a mortgage, so why should you?"

Fred was happy to make it easier and agreed to declare to the Inland Revenue that he had earned all the money in that year, leaving himself open to a much larger tax bill. Even so, the weasel of an accountant was still unhelpful, claiming it would make him look suspicious. Fred decided on the spot to get rid of the accountant, do his own books, and, if necessary, plead ignorance.

Fred paid cash and prepared to face the consequences. He bought a large, newly built house and moved in, once again, without researching neigh-bours. Fred was not cut out to live near anyone, especially without fields and numerous sheds to get lost in at appropriate times. Now he had two air force officer neighbours, one living to the left of him and the other behind the house to the right. That meant these noisy officers could converse with each other in loud voices over Fred's garden. This had to stop. Should he allow them to use the airwaves, his airwaves over his head, especially when indulging in private functions? No.

It was time to give some orders to the officers. He stood on a chair and spoke to them both politely, of course. "If you want to talk, then one should visit the other or don't talk at all. Also, every morn-ing you both have a batman to come and dress you. Okay, but tell them not to park their cars outside my house blocking everything up, or I will move them. Also, you named your house 'Cherry Tree' after the tree in your garden; well, it's not a cherry tree, it's a flowering copper beech."

They did seem to take all that as officers and gentlemen should; time would tell.

The next morning came, as did the batmen and their cars. The batmen were not officers and cer-tainly not gentlemen and took some persuading to move their cars from Fred's front, but eventually, they did. Fred was away all day working only to return that evening. It had been dark a while, and one batman had, under cover of darkness, parked his VW car outside Fred's house and ran off quickly - so quickly, in fact, he had forgotten to lock his car. This road was on a bit of a slope. Fred had some workshop rubber gloves on; he opened the car door and let the handbrake off. The Beetle immediately rolled off down the slope. Fred tried steering, but the steering lock was on, so it kept going straight. It was now going too fast to hold back, and the hand-brake was out of reach. Fred decided to just let it go, thinking it would probably soon stop against a bank or tree, but of course, it did not. In fact, it mounted the first bank and turned over on its side in the road, coming to a stop. Fred, on the other hand, did not stop. He had far too much to do, so much that by the time he finished, he would have completely for-gotten about anything to do with a Beetle and its movements. By now, his neighbours were looking concerned but no longer parked in front.

A few weeks later, Fred and his wife were out at a dinner dance when the oldest daughter decided to make toffee. She forgot it was cooking, and it caught alight. The girls called Henry from next door, who came to the rescue. He arrived, grabbed the pan and pulled it from the grill, then realised it was hot, so he dropped it; the fire was then in the middle of the kitchen.

Fred and his wife arrived home to find a note on the stairs saying, "We are alright. Henry came, and the fire engine came and checked and said the fire is out ... See you in the morning."

As soon as Fred looked in the kitchen, he saw the walls were black. Helpful Henry had cut a large piece of lino flooring from the centre of the floor, and the table was very noticeably shorter where the legs had burnt. Fred just had to laugh; it looked so comical. Anyway, what good would any other action do?

Fred was feeling restless once again; town life, the lack of freedom, fields and sheds and the total lack of privacy were bringing out the Gypsy in him. He also knew how much his girls would appreciate a life with horses and land to roam. Their ages also meant time for a change away from the obvious attraction of boys and drugs. He accepted that the area you were in and the habits of their friends, good or bad, would be corrupting, and if children were bright and adventurous, you could not blame them for being lured into some wrong choices. A plan was made: he would buy a small farm in the popular holiday area of Pembrokeshire, west Wales and set up a riding centre for holidaymakers. Of course, that would mean a lot of horses and equipment, not to mention sleeping and washing facilities for resident riders etc. All this would mean Fred having to stay to work at the old business in England for a few years until everything was established and paid for.

The large house was sold, and the farm was found on the edge of the Preseli mountains. A lorry was bought, and the move started with furniture and horses plus hay and straw; it would take several trips. Gradually it was all done, including the necessary building work extension of living facilities plus stables etc. The buying of enough safe riding horses for the inexperienced was hard and slow, and the holiday season proved short, in fact, not much longer than school holidays. Nevertheless, they had started, and it would be foolhardy to stop now without giving it the full effort.

Fred would have to travel up and down from London to Wales weekly for several more years to keep working at the old, now crumbling business. He just, along with the riding school, wanted any finance to put into it.

It proved to be 30 years before he could sell up and move to Wales to live the dream, despite lecturing at the art college part-time in Wales to help make ends meet.

The first ten years of riding holidays had gone well, but his wife wanted a change. She said she was fed up with smelling of horses and wanted an underwear shop, which Fred duly provided for her. This failed, and Fred joked they should have done more research as it seemed Welsh women in farming areas did not wear knickers, just hay or straw cunningly plaited with the bits of their own natural foliage. Despite all these financial losses, Fred worked on and supplied his wife's next need - a restaurant. This would eventually cause their divorce.

Fred finally sold out the collapsing London business and moved to Wales, taking his sandblasting equipment with him, which was fortunate. After the divorce and settlement, he badly needed to go back to full-time work. He had found it necessary as he had taken out a mortgage to pay off his wife. It took some time to find his feet with his family gone. His wife, of course, had found a boyfriend while he had been working away.

When running a new business in Wales, being English, the Welsh were slow to trust Fred at first, but eventually did and then were extremely loyal. He had been treated really well, where he had coached rugby successfully. This had led to some of the happiest times of his life since the loss of grandparents Harry and Dora. He needed other activities as he lived alone. The three oldest daughters didn't visit him for nearly thirty years; the youngest, the one who was not brainwashed, never failed to be happy and friendly with him. She was away at law school and living a long way away, but her love was greatly needed.

At last, Fred was building a life. He also started playing competition pool, soon to be chairman of the county pool society and captain of a successful team. At this team's local pub, there was an Irish red setter female dog that had just had five pups. Fred swore he did not want a dog, but had secretly fallen for one and had, in his mind, named him. One day, after a successful pool match, the celebrations had led to drinking too much, and the pub landlady drove Fred home. The next day, when he called at the pub for his car, he was told he had bought a dog. They also knew which one and the name he had given it, 'Henry,' so it had to be true. For all his short life, Henry went everywhere with him; work or play, it was a love match.

"Dogs look up to you, cats look down on you, but pigs are equal."

Chapter 14

Fred was finding it hard to continue all he had undertaken. Lecturing at the art college had been an achievement and very successful, particularly as he had blagged his way in with no teaching qualifications, just his personal skills and experiences. In his youth, he spent the summer holidays working with an old relative as a wheelwright and blacksmith, which involved a lot of forge work, coupled with welding and panel beating at his coach works. He had all the techniques necessary to teach students of any age, and no one would be any the wiser. Fred even received commissions while there - weather vanes and large chandeliers for churches - incorporating a lot of artwork.

He gave up this and a lot of horse work to concentrate financially on the sandblasting. He was blast cleaning anything from buildings, boats, lorries, bridges, statues – anything, in fact. This equipment, plus the farm, qualified him to install a large diesel tank and have bulk deliveries of red diesel. With a bit of care and vigilance, this meant that every machine and vehicle would never use expensive white diesel again. All in all, Fred was getting back on his feet - financially, anyway.

One day, Fred received a phone call at 'Blasters.'

"Kinetic calling. Is that Blasters? Who am I talking to?" the caller asked.

He answered, "Fred."

"Well, Fred, are you available to do some blasting for us?"

The answer again was the same but in reverse. "Yes, who am I talking to?"

"This is Colin Davies. I am the manager of Kinetic Pendine, the Ministry of Defence test sites. I would like to meet you here as soon as possible for some prices, mainly for blasting test tracks. One is a mile long, consisting of two railway lines a foot apart with fixing points every nine inches or so for a mile. The other is a single rail overhead track with girder supports every six feet for half a mile, both designed to test guided missiles under controlled situations."

Fred arranged to go to the site. As he looked at the mile-long track, it was mind-boggling; it just went out of sight. He priced it clamp-by-clamp and metre-by-metre, pricing it expensively, then doubled it, added a bit more and then rounded it up.

Even then, it seemed cheap - compared to the opposition - but he needed the job. With a smile, Colin accepted and wanted to arrange a date then and there. With that done, Fred started delivering compressors and equipment. He towed several tons of blasting grit directly from the docks, and he would bring diesel daily.

On the first day, he arrived to be met by Colin, who persuaded Fred reluctantly to start blasting in the middle of the track. The job was hard and slow, but if nothing else, Fred was stoic and just kept going. The other reason was, of course, he needed to be paid.

The first week went by. Colin was pleased and said, "Fred, you can now start at the beginning."

Fred was about to find out why now and not before. There for all to see, was evidence of where other blast companies had started and failed to get men at any price to handle this enormous job. Fred had been told to start in the middle, hoping he would not see the failures and be put off or do a disappearing act. However, Fred was not a quitter. He had invested in materials for this job and wanted to be paid. The grit had come at a good price: Fred had befriended the forklift driver at the docks and was buying directly from him at a quarter of its cost for cash.

In under a month, he had completed the job. Fred was now concerned it would rain, and the surface would rust. He need not have worried; Kinetic arrived with a large fire engine and washed the whole thing off, saying it needed to rust red before they could paint it with their special paint.

"Okay, Colin, you know best. I was only trying to help," Fred said.

As good as their word, they paid almost immediately, and Fred moved on to the next track. It was another success, and then he went back to the ordinary blasting jobs.

It was over a year later when Fred heard from them again.

"Hello, Fred; Colin here. Can you blast our track again?"

"Yes, Colin. When?"

"We will give you a month's warning and pay you 30 per cent more - if that suits you?"

"Okay, talk again."

Fred heard nothing until Colin called again.

"The job's cancelled; the Ministry has agreed to share technology with the French on the understanding we can use their track."

"Okay, Colin."

Six weeks later, there was another call.

"Fred, can you blast the track now and quickly, please? We borrowed the French one, but had a problem with the ignition. It blew up, levelling all their track and site; they are not happy."

This particular missile had been complicated. At the end of the track, it would strike a solid concrete building and go through two layers of very thick concrete, reconstituting the damaged walls behind it to maximise the explosive effect inside.

The first day Fred went to work there again, he pulled up at the security gate and office with Henry, his red setter, sitting on the passenger seat. There was a large warning sign that read NO ANIMALS ON SITE and a picture of a dog. 'Uh-oh, time to act dumb,' Fred thought. Even security knew how important it was to get this track ready. They frowned and waved them through: just as well because Fred went nowhere without Henry. They did, however, point sheepishly at the sign. Fred just shrugged and drove in as Henry leaned out of the window and almost gave the guard a friendly lick. Amused, Fred thought he had got the ministry by the short and curlies. They drove in, and he settled Henry on a long chain under a tree away from noise and dust. Fred started the machines and went to work.

Half an hour later, Colin arrived looking uncomfortable and hung around, embarrassed.

After a while, Fred lowered the blaster and said questioningly, "Colin, what?"

Colin replied, "How's it going?"

"Okay," Fred said, but he knew what he really came for.

An hour later, he was back; perhaps he had plucked up the courage this time to mention Henry.

Fred turned and said, "What now, Colin?"

He replied, "Nothing - all okay?"

Fred said, "All's okay if you fuck off and let me get on."

He went, but at lunchtime, he was back again. It had to be crunch time, so a little sabre-rattling might help.

Fred turned, hands on hips, exasperated and said, "WHAT?"

This time it was different. Colin leaned into his car, lifted out a bowl and said, "I have brought your dog some water."

This was official acceptance: Henry had got security clearance. Despite the sparring, both men knew they had mutual respect.

Halfway through the job, Colin came to explain there was going to be an official inspection of the whole site the next day, and all the top brass would be there. Colin had noticed that Fred had no warning signs around the job; therefore, could Fred possibly take the day off or provide warning signs?

Well, Fred was not one for having days off without good reason, so on the way home that night, he stopped at some road works and took some of their large triangular signs. On each, he painted out the shovels and painted in a pipe looking a bit like a blaster, then printed the words 'Danger Blaster at Work.'

The next morning, he put them in place. Unfortunately, the officers thought they looked comical, and one came to Fred for a quick chat.

He shook Fred's sandy hand and, just above the noise of the compressor, said, "Good to meet you, old chap. Heard about you and your dog. Carry on, damn good man."

Off he went, and he must have said something to the others as now and then, one or two were seen inspecting the make-shift signs with a smile. Some even took pictures, much to Colin's relief.

Fred had a number of rules in life, and he had learned many of them from his beloved grandfather, Harry.

- For every action, there will be an equal and opposite reaction.
- There will always be a good side as well as a bad side.
- It's an ill wind that blows no one any good.
- If it does not kill you, it will make you stronger.
- Winds blow both ways. No matter how hard to find, just look, and you will find it.
- Never start trouble, but be prepared to be a violent retaliator.
- Do what needs to be done - not just because you have to but because you must.

Chapter 15

The good times of blasting were disappearing. Too much opposition was starting up, the riding school needed staff, and the tax man was investigating the part-time art college work. The divorce was imminent, and bailiffs were hounding him, trying to serve a notice on him to stop him from spending any money until a settlement was made.

Fred's wandering Gypsy blood was telling him to move on, so he bought a large motor home. With the latest lady, Rose, he drove off to search southeast France for somewhere to start again. Fred bought a large house with a farm and moved in to develop it into gîtes and rooms to let for bed and breakfast. The gardens and orchards were overgrown and had to be cleared. All the land needed to be fenced off, and his horses had to be shipped over, as did his furniture, quad bike and tools. In fact, several trips back and forth with his lorry and trailer were required.

Fred had all the trappings of a wealthy, retired businessman, never to be suspected of anything dubious. However, the real money situation was money was being spent fast. The gîte and B&B

were not making enough money, so a serious decision had to be made. Fred had always had an idea up his sleeve, and now was the time to use it.

Upstairs, at the end of the house, was an extremely large room with two stories of empty space right up to the roof. The size of four double rooms with large, shuttered windows, this area was entered by a door from the house landing, so it could be a secret workshop. It did not take much imagination to work out that the most productive enterprise for Fred to develop would be growing cannabis or hash, even though he had no experience whatsoever. He would learn he would have to, and if, as he had imagined, it would cost a lot, then he must learn fast, waste nothing and do it all in secret. He had been in this situation so many times before; it was now or never. Time to take another big gamble and do whatever is called for to succeed. All this was going on while he was acting calm and untroubled, like the duck swimming gracefully on the pond; out of sight, its legs are moving frantically underwater.

Fred read and googled every possible fact problem and equipment source, including seed varieties. He made copious notes of all necessities, including electrical requirements. Over the next month, he designed and built grow rooms, a mother plant room, cutting rooms and, of course, fruiting and drying facilities. They were all on timers and automatic watering systems with light systems providing the right light and dark times for each different phase.

At this point, Fred thought he had better attend to his other duties and not neglect the lady, Rose. Anyway, to keep himself mentally happy and satisfied, it was again time to lay Rose, ever-ready and randy, along the back of the Chesterfield settee. She had her panties off as they normally were, legs open and feet comfortably supported by two tall stools, Fred standing between them. He had found this position a year or so and several women ago. It was the perfect height for what he called the lazy man's fuck because it took little energetic thrusting, just steady pushing inside her. Her clitoris was exposed to easy lubrication and serious vibrator work, Fred firmly gripping her by the tits to stabilise her position on the settee. He would not want her to fall off during what would be at least an hour or two's operation. He could use both hands for this as the lady had always taken over full control of the vibrator, only stopping between orgasms while her clitoris recovered its normal sensitivity. A few firm thrusts soon got her back to the main event and another orgasm.

Fred glanced at the clock on the mantlepiece, slightly embarrassed because it was the clock his mother had given him. He managed to put the fact out of his mind; it was dinner time and also time for him to cum or fake it and end this session. This had been the third long session in two days.

Although Rose was extremely attractive and wonderfully over-sexed, there is an old saying, more a warning, that says, "If you are not fucking her, then someone else is."

Well, in this case, there were very few times when Fred was not fucking her. It turned out that when he wasn't, he could hear the low humming of the vibrator, and there were occasional visits to her ex and his hard drugs. Numerous lady friends were involved with her. Luckily, Fred had long since assessed the situation and decided there was not a better option for now and plenty for him at a moment's notice. With full knowledge of what was going on, he decided it was best just to fuck on and not rock the boat. The readily available multiple orgasms should not be sniffed at, well, definitely not sometimes. They were probably hard to replace here in the French town of Mirepoix. He had looked around and found nothing of interest.

For now, it was time for a quick sandwich, finish the workrooms and find a good electrician to connect it all up to the free side of the electric meter. Besides the vast expense of all the electricity needed, a sudden increase in usage, especially of that amount, would raise suspicion and inspection. Fred soon had a dodgy electrician flying in from Poland who understood the score. Although a learning curve, it was now all ready to go.

Five feminised seeds were planted after being in pH-suitable water for three days. Within a week, they had sprouted, and a couple of weeks more, they were a foot tall, soon to be 18 inches tall, with several branches. These are the required female plants that can be safely put under strong grow lamps for a maximum of 16 hours a day. They will grow many strong branches; these will be the mother plants. Over the next month, hundreds of cuttings will be taken and potted. When these are 18 inches tall, they will be transferred to the fruiting room, and the light span will be cut to 11 hours to make these plants believe winter is here. They must fruit, producing large heads or buds of cannabis. The mothers will stay in the grow room, providing a non-stop supply of cuttings. From cuttings to sellable bud means a payday every nine weeks once started. This is as long as a male plant does not get into the system and fertilise them all, in which case, no bud, no payday.

There was a large chimney at one end to connect an extractor to the fumes. The smell was then taken up in the sky, away from prying noses. All the window shutters were kept closed, making it possible to have light and darkness at the right times without people outside knowing. All the ceilings had to be insulated because when it snowed, the roofs over these hot sections would melt the snow in just those places, giving the helicopters that constantly fly over something suspicious to report.

All was underway, and there was just one problem left. He needed an outlet - a buyer to take it all; the last thing he wanted was to be a drug dealer.

Prayers were soon answered. The phone rang, and it was a familiar yet unwelcome voice. Fred had hoped he wouldn't hear it again, and the caller sounded more annoyed than usual.

"Fred?"

"Yes?"

"Can you find someone for us? He is in France, somewhere near Brive. Please try. You know we will pay you well."

"I will try, but there's no guarantee. France is a big place," Fred replied.

"We will send you a WhatsApp picture. His name is Bob. We have a few clues, so we will send what we have." Then they came up with the inevitable inducement. "By the way, we have not heard anything about you lately. What are you up to in Mirepoix?"

This was a veiled threat - if Fred did not help, then they would come to see if they could be a nuisance to him, and he knew they could!!

After asking around and travelling up through central France, he arrived at an old run-down house down a rough track with a lot of commercial vehicles parked. Fred knocked at the door, and it was opened by the man in his WhatsApp picture.

"Hi, Bob. You have been found. Sorry; if it was not me, it would have been someone else. You know what they are like; best pay to get them off your back. You will feel free then to do and go where you like; no more looking over your shoulder."

Bob turned out to be sensible. Fred did not ask how he got into this situation; after all, it was none of his business. An old saying came to mind, "There but for the grace of God go I."

Fred agreed with Bob to say nothing until Bob was in a position to pay them off, and the two of them then went into the town for a beer. By the end of the evening, Fred was aware Bob had a lot of contacts there - nicely away from Fred's. They even agreed to a deal on Fred's produce - a reasonable price so Bob could make a profit, on the understanding he would always pay cash on delivery.

One thing at the back of Fred's mind was that Bob was someone Fred would always have the upper hand over, including physically, should there ever be trouble.

The next day, Fred went to the *'depot vente'* to buy a cupboard which he would use to cover the door to the secret room. He would put casters on it to make it movable and towels and bedding inside it to give it a legitimate use. Now visitors, relations or ladies would be none the wiser.

Chapter 16

For the next ten years or more of growing, Fred would be exposed on a regular basis to cannabis. However, he was never knowingly aware of being high at all, as he had never taken to smoking it. In fact, he did not like the stuff from his first experience. It had only had a mind-bending effect, and the most important thing for Fred was to always be in control and aware of everything around him.

An early experience of this had been provided by a lady called June, who lived in the wilds of Brecon in Wales. She had made cakes with cannabis which led to them being in bed naked and completely befuddled. Fred repeatedly asked the same question because each time he asked, he not only forgot he had but also forgot any answer, if there was one.

His question was, "Have I fucked you yet?"

Evidently, she had answered, "Yes."

Of course, this was immediately forgotten, so they had sex over and over again to make sure. The fact afterwards that Fred had not been in control of his faculties would ensure this would not happen again.

There were far too many serious, if not dangerous, events where a totally clear head was needed. The price had been agreed, including delivery, as he did not want anyone else to know where it all came from. Delivery was dangerous. Fred would change direction several times, checking the rear-view mirror until he was sure no one was following. Also, great care was needed when buying and collecting fertilisers and chemicals. It was very easy for little gangs to follow buyers from grow shops all the way home to their grow rooms and violently rob them of all crops, equipment and cash. Of course, no one could call the police.

What looked like a good crop turned out, by the time it was dried, less than half the weight and value and needed vacuum packing in 100-gram packs and kilo lots. Again, all packaging was considered for security, for example, at Xmas time as Xmas presents. The latest crop was being mixed in among horse feed and saddles.

"Don't employ a pipe smoker."

Fred set off for his 500-kilometre journey with all his usual possible care. Halfway there, he had a call; there was a problem and a different delivery point.

Fred's immediate question was, "Is the money there?"

"Um, er, no, not at the moment," was Bob's answer.

"Well, get it, or I am off home."

"We have some money, and the Pole is ringing around for more customers."

Fred was annoyed and replied, now very agitated, "This is not what we agreed."

As Fred pulled into the new delivery point, he saw a small motor home with a guy known as Rasta and his girlfriend waiting with the Pole.

The Pole had a suggestion. "While we wait for the buyers to arrive, we need to collect a machine of yours, so let's put the stuff in my shed. It will be safe there till we get back. We don't want to get caught with it driving around, do we, Fred?"

"I have a better idea. I just drove 500 kilometres with it, so another five is no trouble. Anyway, I am leaving nothing, especially with Rasta around."

"Rasta is going, so no problem."

Fred was now very angry. "Do you think I am stupid? I trust no one. Nothing leaves my sight until it's paid for."

"Alright, Fred – let's get the machine."

Rasta left, and Fred and the Pole went for the machine.

Once the machine was collected, they returned only to find Rasta back and looking annoyed.

"I wonder what's annoyed you, Rasta." Fred walked over to the Pole's kitchen window. The Pole was on the phone.

Fred listened and heard him reply to the buyer on the phone, "He is a bit over six feet tall."

Fred leaned in the window with his iron bar and said, "You'd better tell him that I am around ten feet tall with this. Far too big for all of you."

Rasta finally came over, bought two packs for cash and left. Several other buyers arrived and bought. Fred had driven all the way there, so he stayed until sales were completed with two thoughts in his mind. Firstly, he would not work this way again, and secondly, how gutless they all were. If they had all got together as they wanted to, although it would be a bit of a blood bath, they would have been bound to come out on top.

Just before he left, Bob turned up. "Sorry I wasn't here; I got delayed."

Fred did not trust him and hit the roof. "Put this right. Do as we agreed at another site without these idiots: you buy everything in one go or fuck off out of my sight for good."

All this had made him late, and after his four-hour drive, when he got back, he still had to check all the plants, timers and water levels before feeding the horses. The last job of the day was to feed the ever-hungry and demanding vagina Rose had already prepared.

Fred had made another discovery: all those that bought cannabis also needed Golden Virginia tobacco for rolling. Well, Andorra was close and sold tobacco for a third of the price. Fred regularly travelled there with a friend Ricky and his wife, who were heavy smokers, so, this time, Fred would be bulk-buying rolling tobacco.

On this occasion, they would go in Fred's motor home. For a start, there were more places to hide things. Ricky and his wife were very against cannabis, so they knew nothing of Fred and his growing, but they both wore layers of combat clothes to happily conceal two thousand cigarettes to bring back over the French border.

A nice easy trip up the mountain to Andorra led to Fred and Ricky buying vastly over the legal limit of tobacco allowed. The motor home was an Aline which meant there was a double bed on springs that let down over the driver's area. Fred lifted the mattress, packed the square boxes of

Golden Virginia in tight rows and put the mattress back on top. The newly bought alcohol was stored in the kitchen area. All loaded, the three of them headed for the border and home. The border was reached, and it was fingers crossed that they did not get stopped and searched. Nearly through and a border guard or *douane* border police stepped out with his hand up. "STOP!"

They had to stop with a bit of a jerk. This was quite a big vehicle, and on stopping, it rocked forward and back again, and the bed came down a little. The guard beckoned Fred and Ricky out, and with worried minds, they did so. "Anything to declare?"

Ricky stood there like a Michelin man with his extra packages.

"Nothing," they both said. They turned to look at the motorhome, and neither of them could stop laughing. When they had stopped, the extra tobacco lowered the bed a little with the jerk. They both saw the exposed front row of Golden Virginia showing - as if it was a bus, and that was where it was going.

The guard said, "Why are you laughing?"

"No reason," they replied.

The guard had seen nothing, and after making some plausible excuses, Fred was glad to drive off.

By this time, Rose had become fidgety and very demanding; her excuse was the need to go back to the UK and her family. Fred never let on that he suspected, quite rightly as it turned out, that she was missing the ex, his hard drugs and also the sex with her established lady friends and their alternative attentions. Firstly, Fred thought a break from her would be good; secondly, a thunderous good-bye fuck would be appreciated; thirdly, it would be good for her to get the female attention she needed. If she came back with a few medical checks, she would be ripe and grateful for the sex Fred would give her; by then, he would need it! Also, her being out of the way for at least a month would be useful business-wise.

Right now, his response was to run upstairs to get the lubricant and vibrator.

"See you in 15 minutes with your knickers off on the settee," he told her. This was just enough time to wash all important parts, hoping she was doing the same, before one more big performance and then "Bon voyage, Blondie."

After the ugly beginning, when at least Fred made sure they knew who they were dealing with and there was no chance of messing around again, all went reasonably well with Bob and his buyers.

Fred was still learning, improving and also ever watchful. If he went to town, he locked everything securely. Often, when he was only halfway there, he would turn around and slowly go back to check no one was hanging around. When in town, he would chat happily, giving off the aura of a comfortably well-off retired gentleman.

At least once a month, he needed to go to the suppliers for nutrients and bulbs. He was always aware of the cars around, particularly on the way home. He would change his route, never going directly home. Some people he knew in Bristol who had walked from their supplier to their house grow rooms were followed, badly beaten and robbed of everything of value. Fred was not going to be caught out in the same way.

Chapter 17

Fred was an early riser; he liked to be on-site as much as possible to see the pumps etc., switch on and off automatically as they should.

One morning, by 6 am, he had checked some lights were on and others off. A lonely day was unfolding. He had his coffee in his hand and walked out through the French windows into the garden. Fred was looking up at the golden aerial bird and tripped over a soldier from the nearby foreign legion barracks. With his gun in hand, he was lying on the ground, looking across the valley to the village. Fred picked himself up and looked around. There were soldiers everywhere and dozens of military vehicles parked up his drive. Smoke and bangs started in the village: it was a mock battle called 'The attack and defence of the town.' Fred's farm was a vantage point for the attackers. All the officers were French, and the soldiers were all foreign, but they were only allowed to speak French.

After Fred's initial concern, he struck up a conversation with the officer. Fred made him coffee, and he needed advice on the best way into the village without being seen. This was easy. As Fred pointed out, he should go down the side of the orchard to the large hedge. Stay under cover of this hedge for 400 metres, then turn left up a winding lane to the village centre. One slight comical hitch was that there were three large, very friendly horses in the field. They were so pleased to see these new friends they ran to say hello, but the troops panicked and ran away, which pleased the horses even more. The officer laughed and stayed for his coffee.

The battle went on all day, with planes flying low over the scene. Fred recorded some and phoned friends to listen over the phone. Many of them had been frightened most of that day by the horses or, like Fred, by the sudden appearance of the soldiers surrounding his house with its naughty secrets they would never know.

An hour later, it was back to normal, which meant listening and watching for helicopters and nosy, unwanted visitors. Also, the *chasse* were the local hunters who thought they were entitled to come onto any land to spend the day with dogs and high-powered rifles, shooting anything: wild boar, deer, hares - in fact, anything that moved. They had not counted on this particular Englishman. Fred had legally informed the mayor when he bought the property that he was anti-hunt.

It took several months and ugly confrontations to convince these arrogant bloodthirsty Frogs that he was not stupid, ill-informed and certainly not a pushover. At the first sign of anything, he was on his quad bike and explaining to the offenders that if they did not go immediately, he would stick their rifles up their butts.

This sorted the problem as, within a week, the mayor had sent two of his hunters, one of whom was his son, to apologise and promise not to intrude again. However, they made the mistake of offering Fred a bag dripping with blood containing, in their eyes, a prime lump of freshly killed wild boar, which Fred politely refused.

"Sorry, I am a vegetarian," he said.

There were no more problems with the hunt.

Fred had three more successful harvests and delivered. Now, of course, Bob and co. wanted to try their arm at getting the price down. This was met by sharp action - Fred said he could take it or leave it, and he would sell it somewhere else. To make it clear, although a nuisance, not to mention more dangerous, he made some phone calls to south Spain and arranged a deal, despite a 19-hour drive into the unknown. It had to be done.

The whole thing was an experience. Driving day and night, worn out, then trying to find the encampment halfway up the Sierra Nevada to find five yurts, some joined together, full of wild, dubious-looking users, was very disconcerting. But now he was here, "On with the show."

The contact man was nice enough but not happy as his wife had left him with very young twins, obviously not impressed with the yurt life. They were having trouble raising the money, and Fred was not leaving without it. Finally, the main man phoned his partner, Leroy, in Nottingham, and he wired him the money. This, of course, meant that Fred did not have to stay another day.

All were wakened in the night.

"THE MOUNTAIN IS ON FIRE!" was the call, and everyone for miles around was racing up to the fields on top of the hills where no one usually went. They were full of cannabis that would all need to be harvested before the fire or the police got there and claimed it. Right at that minute, a flotilla of vans, lorries and trailers were racing up and down, filled with loads of huge cannabis plants, all of which would have to be spirited away, trimmed, hung and dried as soon as possible. This was a big operation; a lot of bud, nowhere near as strong as Fred's, which was grown with nutrients under intense grow lights. The wild outdoor crops only fruited once a year, whereas Fred had a dozen crops or more in a year and would be flown from Granada to Nottingham in suitcases. Luckily, he would not be delivering to yurt town again. It had to be delivered, and no one in yurt town had a license because everyone was banned.

All day driving to Andorra was bad enough, but snow on the Pyrenees mountains was tricky. Chains on, then off for tunnels, then on again out the other side. Thank goodness the French connection had had a serious problem, and they did not want to miss any more harvests. It was now Fred's turn to make demands. He would keep the price down, but from now on, Bob would have to collect cash in hand. He reluctantly agreed because he had to and then wished he had not tried to make demands as he had ended up worse off. No more Spanish trips for Fred.

One unforeseen problem that failed to be recognised was the electricity fuse box. Although large, it was only ever warm, yet the main box downstairs had got hotter and hotter. When everything in the workshop upstairs was on, it was too hot to touch. Fred spoke to as many people as pos-sible about this problem, including the Pole and did not get much helpful advice. Fred tried dividing the times of use to lower the load at any one time. He checked they were not too hot and went to town for a doctor's appointment. All was okay medically, so he drove home. He was within a kilometre when he could see smoke billowing out of every window, door and roof tile. From this, he thought, there would be no chance of saving the house.

He parked away from the house, behind the barn, and ran to the house dragging a long hose, still hoping to save something. He did what he could to douse the flames. He could already hear the main electric cable crackling and flashing as it burnt back along the front of the house. That meant there was no longer any live electricity in the house. He would have carried on hosing, except the hose had burnt in half.

For a while, he changed ideas. Handkerchief over his mouth, struggling not to choke, he ran upstairs. He stuck his head out of a window to get some air into his lungs, then forced his way into the grow room. Fred switched everything off, came out, closed the door and pushed the cupboard up to it, concealing any possible entrance. He took a gulp of air, fell down the stairs, and hosed madly with the half hose left. There was still a lot of smoke, but the flames had gone; it was mainly just smouldering as he went out the back door. There stood the mayor and his son. They had called the fire brigade and electric company an hour before when they saw the fire from the village, but they had still not arrived.

Fred went back into the house and came out as the fire engine arrived, clumsily breaking fences and gates. They also broke up some tiled floors, the excuse being the need to check all was out. The electricity company had switched the power off before they came, and now the *police gendarme* had arrived.

"Is there anyone in the house?"

"No," said Fred, but even so, every official there put on breathing gear.

There must have been 20 officials in the house at any one time. They opened every door and window and searched every room. Fred was among them with his now clogged hankie, attempting to see what they were doing and trying to make sure they did not find the secret door or rooms, which they did not.

It must have looked odd Fred inside with them all the time, and how did they not notice that the house upstairs was only half as long as the downstairs?

After a lot of shunting around, cutting up the grass lawns and breaking the orchard's branches, they went. Some promised to return in the morning - a technical inspector along with electricians to hook up a temporary supply and police for a statement.

This meant Fred worked until early morning to cover any tell-tale tracks or unnecessary wires. After all this, of course, all the cannabis equipment etc. would have to be removed. It was going to be a major operation, but Fred was unsure how thorough the insurance inspector would be. He could not take a chance of them finding a reason not to pay.

The fire and electric inspectors came and could not be bothered and soon left. The next two weeks involved stripping all out with a 4-track and trailer and hiding well out of sight of the house.

Two weeks after that, the insurance inspector arrived and went away happy and satisfied.

Chapter 18

A temporary supply of electricity to the house was connected to make it liveable. It had been cleaned throughout, but it was still depressing. Time was dragging on, waiting for building and repairs to start, but rebuilding all the work areas was well underway. The design of these was much better than before as so much experience had been gained. This time it would be a series of automatic conveyor systems needing little work up to the point of harvest. Everything was designed and built in by Fred, who, once again, would be the only one to know it was there.

Building and decorating work was now underway. It would take another two weeks to complete, including a total rewiring; this time, everything would be better and safer than before.

'What a relief,' Fred thought, 'it would be to live without a lot of the previous fears.'

The fire had initially seemed like a disaster, but now appeared to be a blessing. The old saying came to mind, "It's an ill wind that blows no good," and his granddad's words, "There is always a good side; just smile and look." Well, Fred did, and it wasn't hard to find.

Another major decision he made was that he would no longer transport or deliver anything. He had done, in the past, to be helpful, but in return, he received nothing in the way of help. Yet, at any time, he could have been stopped and straight away returned to the house and disaster.

"Always look for the good side."

Once again, Fred was aware he had got through another possible disaster by staying level-headed and being prepared to do whatever was necessary without hesitation, whatever it had to be.

Now for some good times again as his family had shown signs of visiting. More of a problem was that Rose had arranged to return with her bi-sexual daughter to stay for a while. Unfortunately, the daughter's "while" would get longer and longer until enough was enough, and she was told to go. One of them having to leave meant both of them going. Well, fair enough, goodbye, and that's what happened. Fred was finally fed up with his share of attention, and the duo continually out, hunting any form of sex. It was supposed to be a secret, but it was easily exposed if they were quietly watched for a day. There was a fuss, of course, but Fred had been on top of this possible situation for months. He was past caring and only saw their antics with amusement.

Fred was unused to internet dating, and the thought of a serious relationship or marriage had brought Benny Hill's saying to mind. "Why buy a book when there is a thriving lending library in the town?"

His first meetings from these sites for him just seemed like a license to fuck worldwide, not just on your doorstep, but safely distanced in case of jealousy or repercussions. Starting with Malta and Ireland, there were a lot who were the right age and attractive. Reading between the lines, they had similar likes and needs - a good time, no strings, easy and safe. Contact emails through the agency and honesty were the key, and mutual satisfaction was the goal,

There was one who turned out to be very different but, in her way, entertaining; her internet name was "Bombshell." In her picture, she was identical to Rose, who was, if nothing else, very attractive. This lady was around 50 kilometres from Fred. They spoke on Skype a few times, and he was a bit put off by her saying how upset she was at losing her last partner. They had been called the golden couple as they were both very blonde and attractive (supposedly). Unfortunately, when he contacted her, the Skype picture was always dark. Then she mentioned the boyfriend had committed suicide. Fred was put off a bit but intrigued enough to go to meet her at her house, only an hour or so away.

He arrived anxiously, stopped, got out of his driver's door and looked over at her standing in her doorway. He should have said nothing, but in shock, words came out of his mouth.

"You are nothing like your picture."

She smartly replied, "I don't find you attractive either."

Fred said again, without thought but in total honesty, "At least I am not in drag."

She exploded. "Fuck off, fuck off, fuck off!"

Fred had obviously hit the spot. He drove off but had to stop just out of sight to try to stop laughing. He drove slowly home; he had had his entertainment, and now he would arrange to meet Yvette from Malta for better times. She had arrived, and her friends had collected her from the airport.

'Very handy,' thought Fred. 'This is good, almost delivered to my door.'

She spent the first night with her friends, and they loaned her a car to visit Fred in the morning.

They got on well, and by midday, she said, "I have to go to my friends tonight but would like to go to bed with you."

"That's okay," Fred said, "just tell me when."

"Now," she said without hesitation.

Fred looked at his watch - it was 2:30 pm. "Okay, now then; it is my bedtime," he said and smiled.

They took a short drive home and then had a quick look at the horses, chickens, fruit trees and cat.

As they trotted upstairs once indoors, "That's the bathroom," he pointed out on their way past, knowing it would be needed sooner rather than later.

The bed was clean and ready. Fred had not been a boy scout, but nevertheless, he was always prepared in every way, both in and outside of bed. Foreplay?? Well, you could have called it 100-play or 1000-play; that's how much Fred enjoyed it. Plus, he wanted to provide this lady with an abundance of it because, like all the others, she was happy to play and play all day. This lady also had not been over-used or sexually abused; in fact, her vagina was very trim. He told her so, and she loved to hear it.

He then said, "If you don't mind, I will call you Diva."

"Why Diva?" Yvette inquired. She didn't expect the answer she received, but she really loved it.

"Because you have a perfect, designer vagina."

She beamed and said, "I like the name a lot."

"Diva it is, then."

Fred had achieved what he wanted - his ideal to guarantee a fantastic performance. She was well and truly brainfucked with erotic sex talk, primed and ready, and proved outstanding for the next three hours. The scene was set for the week, and they had not even got to the Chesterfield yet. He also made a point of keeping a few special tricks up his sleeve.

The settee took up most of the next two days, and the first day's brainfuck was far from wearing off. He had hit all the right spots, but it was time for her to go back to Malta and for Fred to get on with his growing work.

Chapter 19

It was harvest time again, and every two weeks after drying, there was a final trim and packing every two weeks. The good life was back - four hours a week on a ride-on mower, daily attention to horses, general farm maintenance, plus hedge trimming down the 400-metre drive, amusingly named 'Knicker Alley.' It is so attractive that every lady being brought down halfway, at the first glimpse of the house, their knickers would be ready to come off voluntarily or already off.

The next vehicle to come down this drive would be Bob coming to collect this month's crops, but first, Fred would drive him up to Andorra to buy cheap tobacco and booze. It turned out to be a nightmare. Near the top of the mountain, it started to snow heavily, and the wind made it worse. Even in Fred's 4x4, they were sliding in all directions, and it fast became a whiteout. There was no way of knowing where they were facing, so they stopped and put on wheel chains. God only knows how they managed to stay on the road, with only the occasional depth pole for guidance - if you could actually see one.

The trip home started okay, but it snowed massively again until most of the way down to sea level again. Many parts were too slippery and icy to apply the brakes, so Fred needed to use the barrier and roadside banking to rub against to slow the 4x4 down.

Bob was happy he had got his tobacco and booze. He was now washing the bags of fingerprints, ready to store the harvest behind the van's panelling for the journey back to Paris. A comical part of this was, once back in Paris, Rasta, who lived down south by Fred, had no idea Fred lived there. He had to drive to Paris to buy, then drive back down again to sell it, meaning at least 1000 kilometres of a pointless journey.

This amused Fred, who said, "It could not happen to a better person."

Another few crops were collected, and soon Diva would be back for round 2, and so would Fred. The next few days would be a welcome blur. As soon as Diva heard her new name, she became naked, displaying her namesake. She became wonderfully sexually demanding for more than a week at a time, and it would be a problem, intruding on work time, to say the least.

'Keep her happy for a few days, pretend to get some hash from somewhere for her, then hopefully, she will be out of it for some time to give me time to do my work,' Fred thought also.

Anyway, the Irish lady, Jean, was to arrive in a few crops' time. Hopefully, she wouldn't be as aggressively sexual as Diva, although he was in need of female companionship, not to mention sex.

Ryanair flies in, bringing Jean, and Fred is there to meet her. He watched her walk across the tarmac, thinking, 'Yes, that's her; another nice but sexually needy person.'

She was straight out about it on the drive home, long before Knicker Alley. Yes, sex was great, and she insisted on telling Fred about her first orgasm, achieved at a young age while straddling a gate. The top bar was rubbing on what she would come to learn was her clitoris. Her body was developing, and she discovered what it felt like to have that part stimulated. She must have been ready because it did not take long – a few rubs, and something strange was happening. The orgasm that till then had been some sort of mythological experience that probably would not happen then did. From then on, Jean searched ravenously for more. Sometimes they happened, but more often than not failed, and so far, they were never as easy as the one on the gate.

It did not take Fred long to realise what she needed. First, a gentle sex talk, then as they were approaching the house, the full-on brainfucking began. They went straight into the sitting room; he pulled her pants down, and she skipped out of them. She was so ready. He picked her up and laid her on the back of the settee. With his trousers down, he stood between her legs, looking happily at her pussy. Being looked at like that obviously thrilled her.

At this moment, he dared not touch her, and foreplay was this time out of the question; she was more than ready. Fred held her by the ankles with her legs apart. He had only just about got half into her before she had one of several screaming orgasms that would come over the next couple of hours.

"How did you do that?" she asked.

"It wasn't me. You did it because you were ready and so capable. But we're ready to find more appreciative and thoughtful things. Make sure you are really ready, body and mind, or don't bother; it's a waste."

This was a really nice but neglected lady - the type that would get hurt. As much as he didn't want to, Fred knew he needed to put himself across as a thoughtless user. The last thing he wanted was to let her get involved or be misled. He wanted her to have a good time but be happy to go home. This Fred hoped for, which she did, and he never contacted her again.

It's been over ten years now since the first crop, and although still a good and reasonable occupation, Fred was getting older. The farm and garden were becoming more hard work, so it was time to sell the farm. Property was not selling easily, and although the price was reduced, there was not much interest. When there was, it was difficult to keep buyers from looking in the grow rooms and still explain what a great and large property it was, plus all the possibilities that could be performed on this site. The other issue was that people would arrive not announced to poke around the property as though as it was for sale, they had a God-given right. On the one hand, Fred could rudely shoo them off, but that might make them suspicious and give him problems.

It was not long before there was an issue. A strange-looking man was looking in the outbuildings.

Fred called to him, "What are you doing?"

He replied, "This is for sale, isn't it?"

"Yes, through an agent. You cannot just show up without arranging it first," Fred replied.

However, he was not going to be put off and said he was in a group of people that would be interested in buying.

Not wanting to upset anything, Fred said, "It's not convenient; in fact, it's very inconvenient, but I'll give you a quick look, okay? Then if you want to come again, make an appointment with the agent, okay?"

Fred showed him around, and inside, the man made some strange comments. One was that his girlfriend called it the plant house.

"We have a lot of plants in the garden," Fred said.

"Where?" he asked. "Show me."

When shown the garden, he said, "No, not these."

After overstaying his welcome, he finally left, driving off towards Toulouse.

Fred could now finish his work and go to bed.

He woke early, and as usual, it was raining. He finished all he could do inside and decided to go to town for an hour or two. He drove up the drive 400 metres to the gate, and there he saw a man in the middle of the next field, walking towards his gate. He turned to walk quickly away.

Fred stopped and shouted at him, "Oi! Come here. What are you doing? Where do you think you are going?"

The man turned to him, and it was the same one as yesterday. Fred grilled him sternly. He had left his car nearly a kilometre away from this field. He had only one weak excuse: that he was a buyer and needed to see more.

"Okay, if you are going to make an offer, jump in," Fred said, gesturing to his vehicle. "We will go back so you can see everything."

That is what they did. He saw all he had seen before, with Fred carefully making sure he did not see too much. This man was trying to think on his feet and stupidly asked about woodland and footpaths as his group did a lot of walking.

As helpful as ever, Fred said, "Yes, I will show you the woodlands. Get in the car."

They drove up the drive to the road where the man said, "I believe you; just drive me to my car."

"No," said Fred, "it's no trouble; I will show you."

"No, my car will do," he said, trying not to protest too much.

Fred's answer was, "Woodlands first."

The man was now very reluctant. They drove three kilometres to some woodland and stopped.

"Okay, come with me. I will show you the paths."

He now knew there was no way out. Fifty metres on, out of sight of the road, they stopped again.

Fred's mood changed. "Now, shithole! What's your game? You came sneaking around my property - uninvited - twice as though there was something to find. Well, as you can see, there is nothing, so you must be trying to steal something. I object to sly bastards creeping around here like you were, with your car hidden, walking across muddy fields in the rain, creeping up to my house."

Fred whacked him on the side of his face. He dropped like a stone.

"Do not fuck around with me again. Come anywhere near my property again, and I will deal with you properly - much worse, understand?"

He nodded.

"Now you can walk back to your car. The rain will cool you down. Luckily for you, I am not taking your shoes. Think yourself lucky."

Fred got back into his car and took his gloves off. He had always worn gloves for times like these as bone knuckles can get damaged, and gloves stop bruising and cuts. You never know who might turn

up interested; that man, turning up like that, probably had plenty to hide as well.

Fred had already decided it was time for a
change; he would soon close the business down
and sell the rest of the horses. Since he was a boy,
Fred had owned nearly 200 horses, and now he was
down to three. Fiffi was the nicest-natured horse
he ever had; her mother, a huge shire, the willful
but wonderful April, and Fiffi's younger sister,
Princess Mini.

A family travelled from Bordeaux to buy Fiffi.
They tried her and bought her; they then saw her
mother, April, and bought her - again without question. Although upset to see them go, at least they
were going together to a good home. An American
lady bought Mini and took her to Nice. Now all his
horses had gone, Fred knew he would never own
another.

He had been involved with horses since he was
born, first with his grandfather and grandmother.
They worked the farm with horses alone for a number of years. He bought horses for all his children,
moved to Wales, bought a riding school and many
more horses, and then started selective breeding.
Now, 80 years later, they have all gone; no more
horses.

Henry, his dog, broke his heart when he died, so he never had another dog.

Fleure - last but not least, love her; this naughty but beloved tortoiseshell cat is still at her home in Cammazet.

GOD LOVE THEM ALL

9 781802 278675